THE LATE HESPERIAN

THE LATE HESPERIAN

TASSO DATTENBERG-DOYLE

First published 2019

by Zuleika Books & Publishing

Thomas House, 84 Eccleston Square
London, SW1V 1PX

Copyright © 2019 Tasso Dattenberg-Doyle

The right of Tasso Dattenberg-Doyle to be
identified as author of this work has been asserted
in accordance with sections 77 and 78 of the
Copyright, Designs and Patents Act 1988.

British Library Cataloguing in Publication Data

A catalogue record for this book is
available from the British Library

ISBN: 978-1-99-962327-2

Designed by Euan Monaghan

Printed in England

1

There is a chapter in *The Magic Mountain* somewhere, where Thomas Mann discusses time. It comes after the reader has followed his protagonist, Hans, up to a sanatorium in Davos in the Swiss Alps. On arrival, Hans hadn't felt very sick, but he gets more sick and must stay. Imperceptibly at first, the days begin to shrink through weak health and inertia, then stasis follows.

Mann writes that repetition abbreviates a life as time's passage blurs and memories spoil. He explains that though memory is a passed world, it needn't be lost because we can enrich the memory of our time. We can seek novelty and surprise, which impress more vividly in our recall, so time's passage and our lives gain breadth, concert and definition.

I thought that was a nice idea when I read it in a cheap room up in the Central Highlands of Vietnam. It occurred to me then that this notion had been in me a long time before I left home, because I'd long felt weary and flat, and the DNA of Mann's epiphany is somewhere in that.

In the second district of Saigon, there is a restaurant called the *Relais Imperial Lê*. The restaurant is the best in the city, renowned for its inventiveness and for menus that are a triumph of the imagination, floating between seasonal delicacies, Vietnamese and French cuisines. It sits on a wealthy street well-known as a foreigners' enclave. Diners leave the main road and traverse a narrow alley; the *Relais* is at the end inside an old, yellow French building with ornate Vietnamese decorations of serpentine dragons and the corners of its roof turned up like elf shoes. The building always looks like it's sweating, because the heavy rain has driven tracts of dark grime through every crack in its bright walls. Inside, it is a mix of a Parisian brasserie and the traditional timber work found in Hoi An, all of it painted in dark hues. Stripes of yellow crossed the dark ochre, brown and black, so the room gloomed around me as I read the menu.

Entrées :

Pâté de lièvre mièvre
Le clocher de Bái Đính de saumon avec ses rondelles de citron
Verdance et porcenelles enrobées de vinaigrette maison

Plat principal :

Confit de canard chou, laqué en rouge

*Le lac Hoàn et son boeuf
Miracle*

Desserts :

*Église de meringue et crème anglaise avec
un sanglot de chantilly, plâtrés en miel de
lavande avec carrelage de prunes et corniche
de grenadine
Un faux gâteau
Glace (divers parfums)*

I ate the hare pâté: little bricks of meat squish,
garlic and chilli in bowls of toasted bread; it
made my lips pucker. Then I had the *Miracle* because I thought I should be bold. It was a
crown formed from small sheets of rice paper and
sauces between the folds. The waiter indicated
for me to take caramelized pork from inside the
crown, remove a sheet of rice and lay it on top.
It was trouble to eat, but no misnomer. And then
my dessert: chocolate nut ice cream with hazel-
nut chips and a small serving jug of espresso,
which I paired with a glass of cognac. I poured
the espresso, watching it melt streams in the ice
cream and pool at the base. I dipped my spoon
in to stir the mingling liquid before tasting the
thick chocolate coat, the resistance of the nut
shards and long twinge of coffee. String music
plinked peacefully through the air. The Martell
tingled the front of my tongue, made my jaw
quiver and warmed throat and belly on its trail,

buttressing the peace of my condition, richly-fed and remembering the beautiful forests and plateaus of the highlands.

The colours were still fresh; there were dark and coarse green fir trees which rose up very tall on steep slopes of wet earth and needle leaves. I remembered the lake with heavy mist over it in the morning. It was that mist over the lake, or rather the effect of the heavy air, which stuck with me. It covered everything with a speckled, film grain complexion. The wateriness felt familiar with its slow pitter-patter and spray. It was homelier than the usual heat of Ho Chi Minh City or the torrents of tropical rain that dispersed it. Outside it was coming down, pouring into every nook and cranny, pushing me to unwanted nostalgia. It was unstoppable in that moment, so I drank more cognac to warm up in memory of the cold weather at home.

It was getting to the end of my time in the country and my meal in that restaurant seemed a fitting bookend. The elegance pleased me, as did the good-looking waitress who had brought me my drink. She stood against a wall, sylph-like and straight as a pillar between two red divans. She had a slim, angular, ageless face, broad shoulders and her hair tied up neatly in a bun, but the greatest beauty was in her easy walk, striding on equidistant steps. She kept her back very straight with the shoulders folded out wide. Under the thin fabric of her shiny traditional dress, I could almost make out the cut of the shoulder blades.

4

Watching her and the couples at the tables around me, I wished for company, preferably hers although most anyone would have done. It would have defied all social convention to talk to her, so I didn't. I should be content in my own company I thought, in the harmony of that cold, demure setting.

I was alone at a large, round table lit only by a small central orange light that was not bright enough to disperse the darkness around the edges of the table and its empty chairs. There were such little motes everywhere and between them paths of shadowed floor that the waiters glossed through.

I might have enjoyed this feeling for a very long time, but for an interruption from my neighbour. On the next table, a man poured himself a large glass of red wine, took a noisy gulp and wiped his sleeve over his forehead. He looked over his shoulder at me (maybe he had felt my eyes boring into the back of his head), and sucked his lips, bringing his heavy cheeks in like buttocks. He swallowed the wine, smiled at me and raised his glass. I did the same, acknowledging our silent fraternity as the two loners in this place.

He was a tall potato-ish man. I imagined that he would reach well over six feet, but this had done little to stretch him out. He had a large midriff, a heavy, drooping chest and a stern, chunky head with a thick black tuft of hair on top, which contrasted his burnt ham complexion. I wondered how I had missed the man's entrance and wished I had seen him walk. It would be an amble, one which only achieves locomotion by moving stiffly side to side like a chubby starfish.

The waitress left her post and went to the kitchen, appearing a little bit later carrying a vast plate which she brought over to the man. It was *boeuf à la moelle,* a dish of thick beef bones with fatty marrow that you scoop out with a spoon. They served it with plenty of meat and a bordelaise sauce. The man pulled the plate up to his belly and started. He ate with some difficulty, pushing his face deep inside the concave bone, breathing through trumpeting nostrils and biting more meat as space freed in his mouth. He was very disgusting; I couldn't see if he was enjoying it, but he worked and tore. When a piece of sinew resisted, he strained his neck till it snapped and pulled the meat in with his lapping tongue. The man spilled out of his jumper and shorts; fat and sauce smelted to his sweat, soaking down his face in rills. The noise of this violent war drew everyone's attention. Other guests raised their eyebrows and I saw the astonished look on the waitress' face, which blossomed into an amused smile. He was so disgusting and lost in the meat.

It looked like he would die – any minute – and this reminded me of things further back than Mann, past Julian, this muddy time of booze, back to Vera.

2

It was a high summer in London; one of the best I can remember. Every morning the sky diluted from black to navy, soft blue, tinges of grey and as the sun rose higher, beams shot through it all and gold swelled behind the clouds like a heart. For weeks, there was nothing to do but bask in this glory. I sat in parks and outside pubs with a rotating bevvy of drinkers, swilling, joking and enjoying our unconcerned, washed out existence, knowing that whatever crapula awoke with us in the morning would be dismissed or shouldered with friends in similar condition. We were twinned in sickness and health, so we always found the energy in one another to persevere for another day and night.

Those weeks are rolled up in my imagination like rollmops, and I think of them fondly, but it happened also, I recall with less joy, that a very sizeable portion of my family died that summer. Many of them were not close acquaintances, and unfortunately their funerals would be the most intimate thing we ever shared. Such was the number of dead, that I was sometimes bewildered by who we were burying.

For some, however, I can remember the exact point of hearing the news of their death, which is a strange moment. When my aunt passed away, my father didn't even turn around from his desk; he just instructed me to polish my shoes and pass the lint roller over my black suit. On another occasion a few weeks later, I was returning from the bathrooms at a Peruvian restaurant and found my parents talking animatedly. My mother kept saying that something would devastate her brother, but he'd get a lot of money, and that was something. What's this, or something like it, I asked. A dead great uncle. These deaths weighed heavily on the latter part of the summer and ruined my native frivolity. There were enough funerals that I needed to invest in a better graveside getup. After the third, my mother noticed that a lint roller wouldn't do. I needed a whole new suit because the moths had gotten at mine. I was given the money to have a new one tailored and that wasn't bad at all. I enjoyed it a lot; as we sat on the tube in silence, I'd preen myself in the grey, milky reflection of the window.

So: many died, and some were much sadder than others. My great uncle Michael died at 102 but he had been running on fumes for decades according to my father and in the end, he went the good way. No sickness, not even on his last day; he just slept on. When someone went to check on him, they said he looked quite peaceful in his comfy bed, next to the window that looked out onto a common where people were walking their dogs and children played. Everything else trundles on and rightly so. 102 is astonishingly old and they said Michael's mush of sunken basins and wrinkles, usually prone to crotchetiness and disappointed sighs, looked, in its moment of departure, not unhappy.

After his funeral I walked with my 10-year-old cousin back to the cars and he asked me about my high scores in a video game we both play, and I remember I boasted because I was very good at that game. We had almost forgotten what this day had been set aside for.

At the wake afterwards the weather was still just wonderful, and we ate coronation chicken sandwiches, tabbouleh, crisps, pork pies and the apples from my great uncle's garden. I went upstairs to see where the big event had taken place and saw that I had been well-informed. The room was comfortable but already very empty. I tried to imagine him in bed, but the space yawned in protest. I looked through his old things instead. There were pictures of him in the army when he was handsome, and his face had plump cheeks. There were a few old books, a sizeable pocket knife, three very thick blazers, corduroy trousers stretching the whole gamut from light to dark brown, and a few silvery trinkets that will have meant something to him. I pocketed the knife, one of the books and a little silver statuette. I heard later that the house would be sold to a young family, which I thought was good. The rest of the day was spent in the sun next to a large bucket of water and ice filled with beer and cider.

It was much sadder when we buried my father's cousin Malcolm. He was sick for a long time, and many family members had doted on him and taken him to see doctors, friends, family and his priest during his sickness. My mother told me about the first time she had met him and said he was a joyful man who read, prayed and played a lot of sport. For all his good looks and charm, he had never married (no-one had gotten out of him why), and he kept himself very busy with community matters and groups that he joined. People from all these corners, and a lot of family, were at his send-off. We talked about the sickness and we circulated the last picture of him that had been taken when he was alive. I had only met him two or three times, but I tried to reconstitute his face from the one in the photo which was a ghostly chalk in complexion and texture, his hair almost gone, the sag of his jaw peppered with beard bristle and the flakes of brittle skin that stood up and curled back on themselves.

His service was grave, and we sang his favourite hymn to say goodbye.

Abide with me; fast falls the eventide;
The darkness deepens; Lord with me abide.
When other helpers fail and comforts flee,
Help of the helpless, O abide with me.

Swift to its close ebbs out life's little day;
Earth's joys grow dim; its glories pass away;
Change and decay in all around I see;
O Thou who changest not, abide with me.

Not a brief glance I beg, a passing word,
But as Thou dwell'st with Thy disciples, Lord,
Familiar, condescending, patient, free.
Come not to sojourn, but abide with me.

Thou on my head in early youth didst smile,
And though rebellious and perverse meanwhile,
Thou hast not left me, oft as I left Thee.
On to the close, O Lord, abide with me.

I need Thy presence every passing hour.
What but Thy grace can foil the tempter's power?
Who, like Thyself, my guide and stay can be?
Through cloud and sunshine, Lord, abide with me.

I fear no foe, with Thee at hand to bless;
Ills have no weight, and tears no bitterness.
Where is death's sting? Where, grave, thy victory?
I triumph still, if Thou abide with me.

Hold Thou Thy cross before my closing eyes;
Shine through the gloom and point me to the skies.
Heaven's morning breaks, and earth's vain
    shadows flee;
In life, in death, O Lord, abide with me.

We emerged from the church exhausted. The coffin was borne down the paths of the graveyard, and past the headstones that would be Malcolm's only permanent company from that day. *Dust to dust, ashes to ashes* was recited and, after a lot of crying from everyone, the coffin was slowly lowered into the ground and earth heaped on top. As I watched the earth being shovelled, a long hand reached up and touched my shoulder. I turned around to see my old aunt Vera. I was crying, snotty and red-faced, and she nodded reassuringly and watched the service with me. I stayed for a long time at the graveside and she had to pull on my arm to tell me we should join my parents; it was time to leave.

"What an ugly, cheap coffin," she muttered regretfully and shook her head as we walked back through the paths.

The wake was dispirited. The day broke us all and we sat quietly in Vera's garden. It was getting late in the afternoon and the dark green foliage had the blue numen of approaching evening over it. I helped Vera bring out cases of wine and beer and we resumed our routine drinking. Later my father gave a speech about his beloved cousin, friend to all and curious about all things.

"It was 19--. We had gone down to watch a cricket match at our old school which we attended at the same time. Malcolm was a few years above me, but he didn't keep a distance. He was always helping me and, even then, everyone could see that he was really a... a... forthcoming individual and someone with fibre and resonance. He was a good rugby player, a remarkable batsman, a chorister, he was in the CCF and the head of his house. I was a professional fielder and substitute footballer, so we had very different memories to exchange on the drive down. He had a benevolent disposition and that made him such great company because he remembered everything more fondly and kindly than it had been, and his stories made us laugh all the drive down. We went in my shabby old car and watched the old boys play the new boys in football and we lost unfortunately, as I recall. After the match we caught up with some of the other old boys and wandered down to a pub in the village. We drank until the embarrassing moment when I realized I was too drunk to drive the car back, so we decided to stay the night.

Later in the evening, a man came into this old pub and sat down at the bar. He ordered a pint and a half pint of bitter and drank the full pint thirstily. He was in his 60s, shortish, white-haired with large plates for hands and a friendly face. He was familiar to the others in the pub who nodded to him, but he sat alone. The man kept drinking and talking to the bar keep all about comings and goings in the village and new developments. Against my pleadings, Malcolm sat down next to him and introduced himself. The man told us he knew our school, of course, and told us about run-ins he'd had with our types when he was a kid, but it was all amicable, and we kept ordering more drinks though he never touched the half. He and Malcolm got on very well and exchanged stories all night like old friends. Finally, when it got late, he told us something remarkable... something black from the past, which Malcolm and I never forgot. The man said he knew the village and its history better than anyone and that that pub was a jail where prisoners were kept before they were hanged, so it was a house for dead men, not live ones. We asked what he meant but he just said it again: we were in a house for dead men. He kept laughing and his eyes twinkled a little madly, then the pub man got up, drank the rest of his pint, shook our hands and walked out. As he went, Malcolm called after him and said he'd left his half pint. The man turned around and said "that's not mine. I give it to the dead" and was gone.

When Malcolm's father died five years ago, we got him a beer too and, to me, this was the real Malcolm. A man of deep, informed compassion, who wanted the world to feel warmer.

That day is the fondest memory we shared, and we talked about that night all the time... Hrumph..."

With another tipsy sniff he filled up a glass of bitter and put it on a table. He raised the rest of the bottle and we all said, 'to Malcolm!'. We drank to his memory, ragged and lost.

As evening turned to night, Vera and I were the only ones left. We stayed up longer than anyone else and, when it started to get too cold, we put on a John Wayne film we had watched many times when I was a child. We hummed the songs, laughed at the jokes and felt the excitement of the shootout all over again. We had sherry and

I told her how I'd been getting on since leaving university, which wasn't fantastically, and that I had paintings no-one cared about, nowhere to exhibit them and an overpowering feeling that they weren't very good. She nodded like at the graveyard and kept her hand on my forearm. She said she would help me and said I should sleep there that night. I went up to the little green and turquoise room I had sometimes slept in as a child. It had dark wooden floorboards and an old window of thin glass. I made a hobbit hole out of blankets, curled up and passed out. After that night I saw Vera a lot, and the room became mine once more.

3

Vera looked in sitting like a cat, in standing like a willow, and in walking like a fluttering bird. The versatility of her demeanour sprang from the fine clothing she wore. She kept the appearance of comfort, layering herself with soft, flowing dark fabrics that accentuated her ease in any position. When she sat, she looked sunken and cosy, when she stood, they hung like a waterfall of inks, and when she walked, they wrapped and defined her momentum. Black was her anchor colour because all inks look much the same as black when seen in their bottles; it is only when they are stretched out that the subtlety of the colour is revealed. That's how Vera dressed. I never found out where she had pieced together such a fine wardrobe. It was not in her nature to betray her secrets, not out of malice but out of pride, which I liked about her.

It was a matter of family lore that as a youth she had been remarkably beautiful. After her, those who had a refined jawline, straight nose, and the forehead not too straight nor round and knitted to the hair in the perfect place, were often said to have inherited their good looks from aunt Vera. They said it often about me and my long, dark hair. As she got older and as her demeanour stooped, we complimented her more, hoping to make her smile. She was not cold enough to say the contrary, so she answered with thin smiles.

For a long time, she had sung then she had written, then acted then painted. These activities took her into her late 60s, in which time she had met and even been well-acquainted with some very noteworthy people in London's posh-artistic circles. There were innumerable gallery openings, concerts, readings, plays, screenings and meet-and-greets for her to attend and though she declined most offers, she made sure to leave the invitations on her coffee table in the living room. When these were mentioned, she liked to balk that these were tiny affairs compared to her own work. There were masterpieces to be done, and pieces that would never be understood by others. Such work needed her attention more and, even if they never saw the light of the gallery themselves, the works were achievements of a higher order. Her assured manner, advanced years and imperious countenance left no room for challenge, only praise for one so accomplished. And yet she could be very sweet. When I visited her, I often found that she had invited a friend of hers from the old days, and perhaps their child so that I would have 'someone my own age to play with'. I think this misguided attempt to help came from not having children herself. She only wanted me to be happy and didn't know that the age disparity was not a problem. And invariably her old friends were interesting anyway. They had written books or sold paintings or worked with people in such circles and that's what interested me.

When they asked Vera about her work, they too accepted her answers as we did. In their company, she could flower for a while and revivify. She spoke about the good old days but didn't hint at remorse, implying her own success by lamenting the woes of others. 'Poor thing, Alexandra and her divorce from that awful man' and 'such a tragedy what they said about Henry's latest exhibition. He deserved better.' They must all have known it was a bit insincere.

When there was no-one else, the house felt only like her. Hers was a redbrick home near Wimbledon Common, marked by the greenery and affluence of the area. From the outside it looked neat and cosy, but inside everything was saturated by her changing character. Sometimes it was Narnia, other times Gormenghast. Mistakes were disasters, and strokes of luck were miracles in her world, and she cast fresh rain and shine with every hour. From the moment she swept in, the pervasiveness of her being affected me, so my mood was moulded inside hers. I was quiet when she was frustrated and jovial when she was content, but I knew she liked me to be there, whatever feeling she was in.

When it was us two alone, often we'd talk about her childhood and the adventures of her youth and all the interesting men she'd met. She said she had visited India three times and was supposed to spend a week on an ashram but left before they were scheduled to start, after she learned that there was to be no talking at all during their stay. After that she'd had a spree in Singapore, Kuala Lumpur and Hong Kong.

"Well, of course, it didn't pay for itself. It was either the boys who did, or I'd have to find a way to get the money."

Her lips pursed together tightly for a second and her eyes went glassy.

"In Hong Kong actually, I was trapped when a man in our social circle asked me to visit him there. I told him certainly not, and to call me when he was less drunk, but he said he'd pay for the flight and that it was an inspiring place. I said I didn't need any advice from him but of course if he was paying, only a stupid person would turn it down, so I said I would go and two weeks later I was sailing through the sky to the Orient. There's

18

something so decadent about life there. The air is different and the smell and bustle... It was very invigorating and elegant."

She stopped and took a generous sip of red wine.

"It was lovely like that for the first few days, but the man simply would not leave me alone. He was always trying to touch me and put his hand around my waist, and he pushed me up to a wall and breathed whiskey down my neck in a bar, so I pushed back. But he didn't take rejection with any dignity, so one day he said he couldn't afford the hotel bill for two rooms and that we should stay in the same room. I simply had to leave. I demanded my ticket home, and he said he wouldn't book one unless I slept with him. Miserable bastard, I kicked him hard in the shin and drove my heel far into his foot and his blood came out. I left him howling there, castrated in front of the whole hotel lobby."

She smiled to me but shuddered in her seat.

"I had to find a way home by myself after that. I took a hotel room that cost damn near all the money I had, because I didn't want to risk going anywhere dodgy. That night I sat and thought about what I could do, and I despaired because I don't speak any Chinese, and I had absolutely no clue how I was supposed to get money. I slept out of exhaustion from my worrying and when I woke up, I had the answer: the casinos. I looked at myself in the mirror and straightened myself out then went out bright and early to the nearest one

I could find. I lost all my money in my first hand, so I went to the bar and hung around until some old coot offered to get me a drink. I accepted it, told him to shove off and said I was displeased with the service to get the money back. I did this in a few different casinos until I had enough money to start again. I might have been at it for a day or more, I tell you. I had mad streaks in roulette and, when I got unlucky, I said the table was cursed and played blackjack. One man kept refunding me my loss whenever I played roulette because he laughed so much when he saw my excitement as the ball went rolling. It was so terrifying... and wonderful. I managed to get a ticket to Paris and from there some friends helped me get back home."

I listened to her tale of herself, enraptured. She held her nose high at the end and turned her head to look at me at a downward slant as if to say, "Do you see who I am now, my dear?"

4

To begin with helping my career, Vera asked me to show her the work that I had done recently. I showed her some old photos I had taken and a triptych I had done at my parent's home, where I was living. The paintings were intended as a statement about commercializing art, but I made a dog's dinner: a collection of homages, plastered over with pop art. When I showed Vera, she asked me what I meant by it, and all I could muster was something unconvincing and banal about capitalism. She called it my 'Eton mess' and left it there. Now and then, Vera was harsh even to me, but at least I had proven a point about the damage of commercialization, if only to myself.

Despite that vitriol, she really did want to help. She made calls to various people she knew and tried to find a fit for me. She insisted I needed more exposure and backhanded me hard when she said that the triptych might sell if it got exhibited because "people misunderstood Duchamp's toilet and now they are inside it. So why shouldn't you succeed?"

Eventually a job was found at an art gallery in Mayfair. I was at Vera's house and heard her tell the owner, Rufus, that I had just gone through a lot and about all the deaths and that she needed him to do her this favour now, for old times' sake. She came back into the living room and flung her hair back: "Et voilà".

Et voilà. I went to the gallery a few days later and Rufus shook my hand, thanked me for taking the job and offered condolences for all the dead people. It was like the suit all over again.

Rufus was odd-looking, with a head like an old orange. It was almost entirely bald, the jaw heavily wrinkled, the temples too, and the knobbly veins of the skull pushed out like mountain ranges with an uneven surface. His eyes were hooded and sunken back, and the skin blotchy purple and blue where little deltas of blood vessels were visible. It can't have been easy going through life with that head, I thought. It was fascinating from every angle, but never attractive. To distract from it, Rufus was always flamboyantly dressed. He wore suits of sprightly hues, and round blue metal glasses that are popular with rich older Italian men. To add a dash of youth (youthful to the 30s not 20s), he liked wearing a brand of Spanish leather shoes with a colourful rubber lining around the edge.

On my first day he showed me my duties, limited as they would be. Most days, the job entailed that I sit patiently for anyone who might wander in, sign for post and answer administrative emails. He was quick to explain that most dialogue over exhibitions, sales and acquisitions would go directly through him, and he wouldn't burden me with them because such business required a personal, familiar relationship. But of course, he was still very pleased to have me, he explained, as he had recently started seeing a woman who made great demands on his time.

"She's a sloanie old girl, I suppose," he said. He had a slow and measured idiolect with long upward inflections that let him raise his eyes wistfully with a thoughtful air. "She expects to be doted on and given presents and attention. It might sound awful to a young man like you, with your expectations of feminism and views on the ludicrousness of chaperones and chevaliers, but to me her qualities are not girlish, but regal, and

22

she can be very kind when she's satisfied with my conduct. So, you see, it is lucky for us both that Vera called when she did."

I nodded and smiled appreciatively, almost exuberantly and blurted out a quick, discordant volume of information about how excited I was and my admiration for his career. It was a formality, and Rufus appeared too shrewd to believe this sycophantism, but he didn't say anything and that was nice of him.

"Well, there isn't a whole lot for you to do, as you've seen, but someone needs to be in this room during the day and I haven't the time, really. Sit, look pretty and praise the pieces if anyone asks. I've put a catalogue on the table with all the information about the artists which you should familiarize yourself with."

He showed me the pieces on display and explained that many belonged to a promising young woman he had discovered at an art college. He said he felt her presence everywhere he went in the room. She had such energy, and this had translated into her art and its vibrancy.

The canvasses were all smeared over with thick, muddy reds and purples and blue human figures, some thin and emaciated like stick men, others cloudy and diluting into the background were traced to each other with lines or placed in constellations. One piece was ringed in black; one had a green whirlpool in the centre. Man/Woman; Black/White; Redness/Blueness of a person; Symmetry/Asymmetry; Life/Death; such grandeur.

23

When I finished looking around and returned the artists' literature to Rufus, he asked: "So what made you decide on art?"

I wanted to look thoughtful and airy like him, so I stopped to consider my answer, but Vera's face was already fastened in my mind.

Vera made Adam in me. By that I mean that she moulded the first person I can remember being with any clarity. Phantom feelings of artistry, melancholy and transcendence bear that Adam's spirit. They still revive in me here and there, confirming Vera's continued presence.

It started with the gift of a blue lacquered guitar with a sunburst at its centre and dark edges. It was a gift for my 9th birthday from my parents, who both pursued an educated interest in music, both popular and classical. They had decided early on that we should explore paths for my interests. Up to then, I don't think I felt different from anyone else, but it is hard to know. I enjoyed pretending to be animals and dinosaurs, climbing what was climbable and watching TV whenever I was allowed, and it all passed very quickly.

But on that birthday, I clanged out my first note and everyone 'ooohhhed' and 'aaaahhhhed'. They ruffled my hair and took pictures and it was that feeling that created my new self-regard. I started to take lessons and my parents became more generous with sweets and television whenever they saw me practicing, so it became a trick

I took advantage of, this attractive appendage to my life. Sometimes I would carry it out with me to the garden when we had guests or play loudly when I wanted attention. I once left it in the living room before a friend came over so that his good-looking mother would notice. I don't think there was anything genuinely devious in such behaviour. I was a child with an inscrutable, flighty but all-conquering mood like all children. I'd say there was nothing devious, but I can't be certain.

Because of my playing, Vera wanted to see me more; I was invited to spend days with her at the weekend. She took it on herself to educate my tastes and played all manner of music, asking me which I wanted to replicate. My attention was caught at 'Brothers in Arms', which is still my favourite song. It's foggy, the cloud-breaking intro feels like a rising plinth, then it glides and floats before tightening its fists. The guitar becomes sinewy and taut, the organ warbles and it shudders down my spine. It is a patient song and Vera and I often mirrored our movements as we tracked the music. She smiled as we pretended to pluck the notes and wriggled our heads upwards during the crescendo. Sometimes, I'd arrive to find she had already decided what she wanted us to listen to as she gave me tea and confectionery on a real silver platter. She was proud to look after me so well and took great interest in my ambitions and my life. I talked to her about my friends and animal facts and she listened and mostly said, 'what else?' so I got used to explaining myself in long segments, pulling out my thoughts like a tapeworm to make her happy. Apart from music and art, it wasn't clear what pattern of topics interested her at the time - it's more recognisable now – but talking and eating cake was about all I wanted.

After cake, she'd ask me to show her my progress, and every week I'd be embarrassed as I took out the guitar and stuttered through the same pieces. It confounded me that I always forgot how much I needed to practice until I got in the car to go to Vera's.

"Play me something different, dear. I know that one and I know you play it so well" she said once, and I had to lie.

"I don't want to."

"Why?"

"It's not ready. It sounds stupid."

She beamed and said I was a perfectionist, which was very far from the truth. But then she told me she felt similarly in her studio and it was my turn to beam. My breath fluttered; she was already an impressive old fox then.

Vera wanted me to practice in her house and often told my parents at the door when I left how much she liked to have me there. But I never practiced earnestly. It was a frustrating pursuit, and my parents and others didn't maintain their initial wonderment whenever I was seen with my guitar. I tried playing football and cricket where the entry level was easier. The mechanisms of sport were organic, but the guitar resisted. My fingers throbbed, and the sound was never right, and I couldn't wrap my fingers around the frets and place my fingers on time or remember the required placement. I struck the strings repeatedly and tried to place my fingers, then I tried placing my fingers then striking the strings and every which other way that seemed sensible. It wasn't good enough and after months passed shirking the instrument, I lost patience. Instead I took to sitting in Vera's conservatory, which she had repurposed as a studio, and watched her work under grey clouds, sun blue skies and a day I remember for hailing so much we thought it would crack the windows.

I cannot remember all the different things she made anymore. I have images of murky canvases with gelatinous figures and bright dashes, pottery flowers and mushrooms and a papier-mâché dog's head I nicknamed 'Meats'. For a long time, she didn't let anyone in with her and the pieces weren't seen for many years. At that time though, I wanted to be like her and paint as well. That's where I began. She would set me up next to her with an easel, or I would sink my hands into clay as was my preference. It was very satisfying to slosh so much stuff around and see where I ended up. Vera would sit and petrify in an armchair for a long time, then cut a few lines through her canvas or the moulded pottery, expressionless in her execution.

Apart from two brief periods in Sixth Form

– one where I wanted to be a banker like Charlie Sheen in *Wall Street* and one where I wanted to be a doctor like my father – little else threatened how I was built in Vera's house.

"I've always been interested in art," I answered. "It's a difficult question to answer." I didn't want to be honest on the subject, it would make me look like a child.

"Well, which artists do you like? Please don't say that's hard to answer too."

"My own work," I joked. Rufus smiled politely and I backtracked. "I was recently looking at some American artists. I like Maxfield Parrish and Frederic Edwin Church...Albert Bierstadt as well. The landscapes make you want to breathe deeper. I don't know exactly what I mean by that, but I remember doing it... Harry Clarke, as well. For more permanent interests, I have always liked Hieronymous Bosch and Pieter Bruegel the Elder. I admire them very much. And Terry Gilliam. Sometimes I think his drawings come from the same place as them. They are similar types of chaos."

Rufus raised his eyebrows and lost himself in thought. For a moment he looked over my head in silence, then he said "Yes, I suppose I can see that. Vera did mention before that you liked painting. Is that sort of thing in your work?"

I rattled through my output. Eminent in my recollection was a piece I had taken out to look at that morning. It was a woman of all buttocks and thighs with fat hips, breasts, red hair and a black and pink background. She was a giant, lying on a bed far too small for her, and underneath the bed, in the dark, were a bunch of smiling, dirty men, grinning and reaching their hands up the sides of the bed. It was a work of prudish shame, which I had thought controversial and provocative for its sexuality. But it was only controversial to me, the caged prude. It was an unpleasant reflection and I decided again that I didn't want to be so honest with Rufus. He didn't need to know what I thought of myself.

"A bit," I said.

The job never became much more than sitting patiently with nothing to do. Vera and I had supposed when I started that Rufus would be a gateway into this business from the other side of the mirror. He had other ideas, I think, or thought me unqualified to join in the meetings he was having, wherever they were. I was a polite presence in the room, occasionally interacted with by people who walked in, and otherwise left to manage bits of paperwork and keep track of Rufus' social engagements, and his friends' birthdays.

Employment challenged my normal rhythm, even if there was little real work. I could have sat, inert in every way, for hours if I'd wished, but when I did, my mind wandered outside this long white corridor, thinking of what I might be doing instead. It felt like stalemate and the art did very little for me. As far as I could tell, I was oversee-ing a room of vomit.

It was only with great difficulty that I did any work of my own in that period. Whenever I got out my sketchpad or thought of things I should paint, I wound up distracted. Like everyone, I had no permanent feelings, just hordes of con-flicting ones. Sometimes I was regretful in a con-templation, other times sympathetic, but there was no identifiable, durable balance between them, so the projects I envisaged changed and morphed too much to get a handle on anything. Sometimes I would try to examine my thoughts to regain my equilibrium, but I became frustrated with my extrapolations, and aware that they were adding another corruption to my ideas. The mind is the defective detective of itself, I decided. When it stares, it goes cross-eyed. As I sat in the gallery then, I learned to do nothing quite well, stuck in vomit.

5

An evening came when Vera was particularly morose. We had watched a documentary on BBC Arts about a German artist Vera had known, whose work was being reappraised. He had been a painter, mainly drawing nudes, but also land-scapes and buildings which used the geometry of the human body. There were muscular towers and fat theatres, their shapes rounded and taut instead of linear. It reminded me of Alasdair Gray and his pictures in my copy of *Lanark* where flesh looks like doughy stone. Vera had watched intently for the first 10 minutes then offered sherry at the first advert break and continued to drink for the remainder of the program. I drank with her and when it was over, Vera looked glum and dispirited.

"I think," she started and took a little sip. "I don't think they really understood Wilhelm there."

She lay back in her armchair, wrapped up in her usual robes with the sofa blanket around her shoulders.

"You know, I always thought Wilhelm was much cleverer than they made him out there. They were so crass and obsessed with the sexual element of his work."

She pronounced the word 'seksual' with an elongated s that made me a bit uncomfortable.

"He didn't warp the body or mutilate it and he thought cities were humane not inhumane. To him, they were a symbol of human unity, and existence in communality and friendship, not vice and exploitation. No, I don't think they understood him at all there, it's a shame."

I finished my sherry and poured myself another, then refilled Vera's.

"Thank you, my love," she said to me with a quick smile. "You know I think that's all narrative nonsense. They need to make a story for

31

people, even though there is no story to real life. He was a darling; he once drove all the way back to London from Cornwall after I threw a tantrum at a party and demanded to leave. Of course, he tried to kiss me in the car, but then they all did... But he wasn't so sentimental. We were friends for a while, but he moved to Edinburgh with a girl called Molly, I think, or some such fat girls' name... I remember that he wrote for Anteros, maybe you've heard of it? It's the sort of thing you should know, it was clever and arty."

A groan went through me as I felt her leaning on my lack of work and her excitement to educate me. She started glowing and pushed herself up in her chair.

"You know, I've still got my copies upstairs. They'll be at the bottom of that old wicker basket in your room. Go and get them."

She indicated with her finger that I was to go immediately, and I obeyed. I went up the stairs to my green and turquoise room and searched for the basket, eventually finding it under cloaks and scarves in the cupboard. I came back a few minutes later with a stack of old editions, all frayed at the sides and faded, but otherwise intact. She opened several copies and pointed out the people she knew and mentions of her name at parties and her first art exhibition.

"But I gave up exhibitions after that because I never wanted to be an establishmentarian. Other voices will drown out yours" she said.

Finally, she found the copy she was looking for and handed it to me.

"Go on," she said, "read that."

She went into the kitchen to heat up some food and I was left to acquaint myself more with Wilhelm.

We imagine four men walking down a street in Paris on a very good summer's day.

The first one walks through but he's busy or not paying attention because he has either too much or nothing he wants to think about.

The second man walks and notices that there is a wind tunnel, which makes the temperature here very pleasant, especially after a long day of walking. He sees that there is a lot of sunlight and that it cuts a beautiful line of shade that divides the street diagonally. The trees are fine, their green is vibrant, the cafés are busy but not loud, the atmosphere is jovial. There is something very beautiful about the way the doors are painted in deep greys and browns that suit the colour of the benches, lampposts and tree guards on the street. The street names stand out in neat blocks of blue and are outlined in green. It contrasts well with the sandstone. He notices that the people here are very well dressed and thinks how chic it all is. He notices a cat sitting in one of the doorways, hiding from the sun. It watches another cat pass with a baleful glare which then licks its fur. There is warmth to this place and this day and the feeling it gives him.

The third man walks and notices much the same as the second man. He is taken by the same feeling of warmth but, as he's walking, he starts to piece together why it feels so comforting. He thinks the fashion of the people is a sign of civil health. The people are well dressed because they want to be more beautiful, and their elegance is a sign that they care about how they present themselves. The man thinks about the cat and how, in the moment the other cat passed, he looked like a lion watching a competitor from the shade of a tree in the savannah. The blue and green of the plaque are also beautiful and always look vivacious because they are the primary colours of nature. The homogenous street colouration is a reminder to him that the people here have made a conscious effort to build harmony.

The fourth man sees the same thing as the second and third. He thinks that there is something truly astounding about how Hausmann built Paris and that much of it isn't as old as we might think. He wonders about the medieval structure of the city and wishes there were more pictures of it. Compared to London, he thinks, Paris often feels cosy. There are more areas with little streets like this one, and London is drippier. Perhaps he's projecting rain onto London because he's only experienced it once and it was sadly a very rainy week. Coupled with England's reputation for bad weather, his view of London has been marked very deeply. Maybe

London is drippy, but Paris will be Hausmann, the cat, a breeze and beauty.

My dear readers: since I first took to painting in my school days, my interest has been to extract and illustrate 'Wahrnehmung'. No, it's not a made-up name or a muse. It is a German word, similar in usage to the English word 'perception', but with very different implications. Perception is heavily informed by the eye. To perceive something sounds like narrowing your eyes, squinting or deriving some information that, on the surface, was not apparent to everyone. The word can even be used for things that are on the surface. You can perceive something in the distance that was not hidden. Wahrnehmung, translated more literally, is an individual's 'grasp of reality'. Its implications are not physical but highly individualistic, because they signify how one interprets reality, not what reality presents. This is an important distinction, because Wahrnehmung, though used to say perception, is also understanding. To clarify the importance of this distinction, I would like to tell a story.

In the late 70s, it was my great pleasure to befriend one of the world's most remarkable people (I mean that, and don't say it lightly): Werner Herzog.

Werner and I went to the same school in Munich, but we did not meet and become friends

35

until much later. In 1977, I ran quite by chance, into an old school friend of mine in a pub near our old school. We drank and reminisced about the good old days (I was not that old, only 34), and he told me I should come to his birthday party the following week. Also, did I know Werner? Werner? I asked. Yes, Werner Stipetic from school. He now went by the name Herzog and was a famous director. Well, he insisted I come and that I should meet him. I was rising in the art world, Werner in film, and maybe we should finally become friends. I agreed, of course; I had seen 'Aguirre, the Wrath of God' in the cinema in 1971 and was blown away, though I hadn't known who made it.

The following week, I went to the party and, with little drunken elegance, our mutual colleague introduced Werner and me and we quickly got along. We talked about school, an old maths teacher who was an idiot, and of course the girls we had liked. We discussed art and his films and other interests and exchanged phone numbers.

Over the next few years, Werner and I met a handful of times. While we kept track of each other's careers and work, it was not until 1981 that we found a crossroad for our interests. He called me one morning and asked me if I wanted to come to his next shooting location in the jungles of Peru. He offered no remuneration, except those of the soul, and said I should paint from his set and that it would make a good book once the film was released, which would be good publicity for us both. It was a kind offer. Outside Europe, I had only visited New York and Werner's invitation uncovered my wanderlust, which I had neglected so long. What was the film called I asked, and he said 'Fitzcarraldo'. It was a strange word: a Norman surname, passed onto the English, which had then migrated to an Irishman, who took it to South America, where it took a Spanish corruption, and got tagged onto a German actor. I didn't know fully what to make of the story, but I was weary in my studio in Munich and needed some fresh blood in me and it would have been timid of me not to go.

Werner's set was famously a civil war. The lead actor was Klaus Kinski, and he fought like an animal every day and night with Werner. Quiet was brief, and comfort non-existent in our Peruvian micro-society. We sat under sticks and leaves and it rained, and the air clung to us like plastic packaging. We worked on a flooded riverbank and I remember wet food and the constant squelch of mud between my toes.

I had arrived during the filming of a key scene. Kinski's character must transport a ship up a mountain, a task no easier to perform than it was to reconstruct. Werner had a ship built, and then it had to be brought up the mountain slowly on logs like the caterpillar tracks of a tank. Kinski's character was mad, madder *than Kinski supposedly, but I couldn't see how anyone could be madder than Kinski or Werner at that time. I helped on set every now and then, but my job was still to paint.*

My work to that point in time was about the artificial human. I did cityscapes and identified or drew the human forms out of these with success, but I wanted a change and reinvention (of my own perceptions). I had become aware, before arriving in Peru, of a recurrence in my thought pattern. Images and notions fell along the walls in my head, reached my attention; I tried to articulate them into my work, then they floated back up to my mind's ceiling, rebounded and floated down again. It was incessant and untenable for a man who works alone. My own company became painful and overfamiliar.

It reached a climax when I started recognizing my own thought patterns in my dreams. I would dream I was on a street and expressed surprise at the strange things I saw there, then asked how I could be surprised about a creation I knew so well, and the ludicrousness of surprise in a world I created and revisited enough made me sick. My inquiries into myself got nowhere, so it was a godsend to leave and air out the mind.

I tried to reverse my artistic ideas at first. The city had reinvented the nature of man. It was a creation with the purpose of ease. Elevators, electronics, roads and neat geometries were ergonomic designs for ergonomic man.

The people were fat with ease, they worked with their minds to calculate and coordinate, in environments that provided the least distraction. Neutral whites and greys were democratic, dull, but efficient choices for our lives. What vigour could flourish in that space was my obsession, until I was in Peru.

Here the world was not moulded to accommodate us, we were moulded to live in it. The young people were slim, their bodies built with angles and accents of musculature that showed purpose and durability. In contrast, the big muscle men like Schwarzenegger, became vulgar to me. Their build was artificial, focused on an aesthetic idea that upset the balance of a body with its natural purpose. Their legs cannot run, their arms cannot fight, their breasts swell and plastify until even the milk is stoppered. In Peru, I saw a new type of body, represented by the harmony of purpose and health. I sketched the young bodies, apt for the world and sex and hunting. I sketched the timid old bodies, cowed by frailty. We are much more aware of our bodies when they stop responding to our will, I think.

My great piece, Werner made clear, should be the ship. It was a collection of timbers with men hacking and plastering it day and night and the forest, its sustenance, was not a stone's throw away. It struck me as a subject for its oppositions. Film, the great fiction of the modern era, stood in contrast to the earthier lives of the locals. In some ways the ship was the city, a creation of natural substances to human designs.

I painted at night and used the dark as a bridge, mixing where the timber of the ship stopped and the forest began, and silhouettes outlined by firelight. It was a grand and bold piece. I thought it was a sign of the triumph that was coming, for his film and my rejuvenating career.

However great I thought my work was though, I abandoned it after one fateful conversation. The head of one of the tribes became interested in my work. He had observed me on a few occasions but one night he wanted to speak, so I got the translator to help. He said that I was drawing it wrong. In my picture the boat was finished and already up the hill. He kept gesturing with his hands from his eyes forward. The translator explained that the man meant I should draw from the past, from what was certain. What became clear through difficult and lengthy translation was that his gesture, from the eyes forward, was not his way of saying to look at the mountain where the boat was, but to the past. For his tribe, the future is not conceived as that which is in front, but that which is behind. The past is in front because we can see what happened there, the future is blind and therefore at our backs. And when Fitzcarraldo looks at the boat with fear as it is pulled up the mountain, it is not the uncertainty ahead that frightens him, it is the failure he knows from his past.

How worlds differ is difficult to appreciate until such moments.

What does this mean for the men?
Let us assume they have a shared culture, unlike that tribe and I. What they see and the extent of their variation is not so heavily influenced by a divergence of upbringing. Their different views are their innate 'Wahrnehmung': how they grip reality, not based on their culture, but on the balance of their inner animal and their human, as Hermann Hesse explored so well with his 'Steppenwolf'. It is the balance of emotional and intellectual inference.

There is an animal world inside us. That world is instinct, sensation, impulse and vigour. The body is subjected to the phenomena of the world and it elicits a response. This is dance, the feeling of skin, the brush of wind, sex and shivering in the cold. It is the primary reaction and comes without need for thought. Its pleasures and pains are raw, and everyone understands them in about equal measures. Some are more sexual, others more violent and so on, but these feelings are essentially common ground.

The variations are greater in the human. What he sees is not purely sensory but informed by other associations, this way:
The first man sees nothing. For whatever reason, he is too distracted and not fully present.
The second man feels the world as it happens to him.

The third man feels the world and, by process of intuition, understands the feeling it produces in him.

The fourth man feels the world and, by process of intuition, understands the feeling it produces in him. and compounds this with an intellectual pleasure that derives from his knowledge of the world.

The same thing can be said of art. Imagine someone looking at a painting of a bearded old man and finding it pleasing. Upon closer inspection, they find that the artist has found a beautifully sad expression with brushstrokes that emphasize the sunken and hollow quality of the eye sockets. The sockets give a circular movement, subtle shadowing darkens the eyes without making them appear unnatural. These inspire a series of experiences in the viewer. He begins to mark the transition from just perception to perception and understanding.

There is another layer of appreciation, another angle of experience, that he may miss if he does not know the subject of the painting. While the man has been given a moving countenance, the observer is not aware that this instance represents an old king mourning the loss of his daughter at the hands of a murderous husband from an old tale. A vivid background forms around the painting. If the observer reads the story, perhaps he'll find even more material to attach to the painting. What do you see? What does it mean? And does knowledge give us a *firmer grasp of reality or is the past a sort of fiction over the present?*

We don't all have time to develop our appreciation of the world. Many have too much work to do and need comfort and distraction at the end of the day, not the challenge of unravelling their own thoughts.

But for those who do have time and are so inclined: my newest exhibition is on at the Turnbell Gallery in Pimlico from the 16ᵗʰ of September.

P.S. Thank you to the editors for correcting and improving my English.

Wilhelm Steinmetz

I could smell the beef that Vera was heating up, so I went into the kitchen where she was stirring a tagine. She was always a fashionable cook. I told her what I had read, and she laughed haughtily.

"Oh, he was always a horrific elitist. If he hadn't had such humanist views, I would have called it a remnant of an *ubermensch* mentality to draw such distinctions between people. And to class them according to the way they perceive things!"

"Grasp reality, Vera. That's his distinction."

"Well I don't really agree with it, whatever he chose to call it. I suppose I glossed over those things. You know, he once asked whether he could paint me in the nude."

I was reluctant to chase this statement, but Vera enjoyed chatting about such things, and the family connection and traditional reserve never interfered.

"Yes, he was always looking for women to paint and said that he wanted it for reference when he was painting over the buildings and streets and things. I can't even remember, but it's possible that I did pose for him."

The thought entered my mind that some of the bountiful skin we had seen on the television was Vera's. It was so sexual, and Wilhelm had gone to such pains to paint the lines and angles of the body, doing such detailed work on the flesh with shadowing that revealed orifices and valleys. I took a big gulp of wine and let her finish her thought in peace, feeling that if I gave it any attention, it would only goad her on.

"Although, perhaps it was Mary who posed. Oh, it's so hard to remember. We were all so young and free in those days. Anyway, I don't agree with what he says. For me, he interpreted things in such a verbal way. Who wants to spend time asking themselves what they feel about things and what they remember about them? It seems a complete waste of time. We have a short time to live and variety is the spice of life. If I stopped to consider how beautiful the flowers are and how their majesty came from such majestic powers of nature, I would never get anything done."

She pushed her nose up like a spaniel to await my rebuttal.

"Well, I have a little more sympathy for him. In many ways I think that what he says is about inner dialogue, and that seems very natural to me. When I make a decision, I think to myself in words and make statements and ask questions until I have figured out the answers that I need."

"Darling, you should let yourself feel more. The heart has a mind of its own after all."

This seemed a leap to me.

"I don't think the heart has a mind. The heart is the animal he describes."

"Then the heart has a character of its own, if you'd prefer. Would you not rather listen to your heart and your instinct than the contrivances of your mind?"

"They aren't contrivances, it's the instrument of understanding."

"Nonsense! It's all masturbation."

I cringed and furrowed my brow in discomfort.

"The whole thing is nonsense. You said so yourself. It's a dialogue, you're speaking to yourself. So, are you delighted with what you see, or delighted with what you project onto it? Because to me it seems you're patting yourself on the head for having had such clever ideas about things. Do you really think all of those professors enjoy the world any more than anyone else? Or are they just locked up in their heads studying what other people live?"

"He just meant that the most profound appreciation is a balance of intellect and intuition."

"Maybe," she said and turned her attention to

45

stirring the beef. After a few moments she looked back at me.

"You know how people use music to say how they feel? People complain about rhythms and being out of sync or having a sense of discord. Do you know what I mean?"

"Yes."

"Well, I think it tells us an awful lot about people. I think that there is a sort of music to us. You notice it more with people who are a bit dim because it's is less complicated and easier to deconstruct. Francis is one of those people. Do you remember when we all went for a walk and we walked past that farm? He ate pig feed because he thought it would make us laugh and he smiled so vacantly... Whether it was the feed or a misfortune of birth, the pig boy has a pig brain. More swine?" she asked, breaking the solemn stride of her point and topping up my glass with a raspy laugh. It was in those moments that I knew how strongly she liked me. Only with me did she let herself be cruel. But I did not let her false joviality convert me. I wanted to know what she meant so I kept quiet, returning us to what she had been saying and the quiet she had tried to avoid. She started again.

"Well Francis, for all his faults, has a good deal of... *Naturel*. He questions little, is rarely unhappy, knows what he enjoys, and searches no further. It makes him simple company for us, but great company for himself. I don't believe he has much chatter in his head. His way is musical.

He's not good at music, that's not what I mean. But his internal rhythm and his harmony with himself is guaranteed by the fact that he wouldn't hear it if he was dissonant. Let's say he misread a social cue: he would simply laugh and say, 'not to worry' and move on. He might apologize or feel a little ashamed, but Francis recovers and keeps to the present."

She put her glass down and looked at me earnestly.

"You, I worry about more. You talk to yourself too much, back and forwarding and confusing your head like a book. You need a better sense of your guts to know your rhythm."

"I don't think so, Vera. And I don't think I think like a book. There are no acts or apotheosis... We're just lengths of string." I said resolutely. I watched Vera fondly, and was suddenly ashamed to see her face fall. It was my fault for speaking so coldly and I wished I hadn't, although it was true. She regained her composure quickly.

"Do you know Walter Pater, dear?"

"No," I said, and Vera smiled. Whatever information she wanted to impart was often packaged in an odyssey that she told with glassy eyes, as if she was hearing it all for the first time herself. "Is he a friend of yours?" I asked.

"In a way yes, but he's long dead. He was a suffering Victorian homosexual... Wrote a number of very interesting things. He's the one who said, 'all art constantly aspires towards the condition of music', perhaps you've heard that before?"

47

I shook my head.

"It doesn't matter, I forgive you. I'll tell you what he meant." She composed herself and straightened her back. "I'll start where I think is best: Pater said that the most accomplished lives, those 'best-lived' if you could call it that to say nothing of achievements and feats, were lives lived as streams of ardent emotion. Such lives were intense and knew the peaks and troughs of experience, they didn't just hover at the middle band. There was nothing more worthwhile, he thought, than the invigoration of the senses. It's a godless perspective, but then, can you blame him? He was a homosexual, so hardly under the wing of the Church, which makes hedonism a more attractive pursuit, though sort of nihilistic."

"I don't see what that says about music." I said, getting drowsy as she twisted me around these ideas.

"I'm getting there, scamp. Well he loved the arts very much and wrote about the Renaissance and how some of the most admired men of that pregnant time merged their love of Classical arts, Ancient Greece and Rome, to their religion, which was of course quite a task. I remember thinking what a lofty ambition, but then it seems natural. Art is a sibling of religion. That religious men have been artists and artists have been religious men is unsurprising, for their concerns are often the same. Walter Pater said that each of the arts had its own strength, but that music was the matter they tried to emulate in their own fields. He meant that music was the vehicle of the closest interpretation of the untampered experience of emotion. You see when you read anything, or observe a painting, a distance is formed. You have to think about the picture to find an interpretation of it, which means taking an intellectual step. But music isn't weighed down like that, it's immediate. The whole meaning and response to a piece of music is contained in its form. You nod and tap your feet instinctively, your mood lifts and dips without passing by understanding in any verbal, self-reflexive capacity. The substance and consequence of music are the same. What do you think?"

It took me some time to answer. I yawned and went through it. I decided there was partial truth to this. I often found the feeling of my own paintings in songs. The 'Eton mess' owed something to *Money for Nothing* and the men under the giantess' bed were produced after I took an interest in Steely Dan. Their feelings were bound; I couldn't deny this involvement, to myself at least. But did that mean that I was trying to articulate form and content into one? The garish orange was garish like the tits and thighs, I supposed. There was some overlap there at least. But what about the statement itself and the nature of music? I thought of the little classical music I knew for comparison, and hit on Beethoven's 9th Symphony and felt, like all others, the universal admiration for the 'Ode to Joy' and Schiller's wonderful words. The words needed reflection to have their full beauty revealed, but even without these, I felt innately that there was much I had learned to appreciate in music only upon reflection. It was not simply a matter of listening more closely to the details of instrumentation – though of course that was important – but equally I derived great satisfaction from developing perspective on the piece overall. The brilliance of one segment of music is diminished or enhanced by the balance of its context. Certainly, there was an initial, electric reaction, but its significance could glimmer or dull with scrutiny.

"I'm not entirely convinced," I finally said. "I don't think your explanation accounts for the whole experience of music. It's not all immediate. Think back to what we were just talking about. Music might feel more complete even without an intellectual reflection, but the pleasure and intelligibility of it grows with understanding, not just sensation. It will always be felt, but reflection will reveal intricacy and substance, or their absence. Remember the 9th -"

"You always mention that piece. Is that all the classical music I showed you? Is that all you remember?" She breathed deeply. "I can see what you mean but you're turning me away from the point I wanted to make. What was it?"

She took a gulp of wine and put her hand on her neck as if she was going to strangle herself. She took some food and chewed slowly, before finding it.

"Even if you only agree partially then, I'll still tell you. I've been thinking about this observation

50

for a while and it has made me think about how it applies to ourselves. People, I mean. As I said, Francis has very little sense of discord. His constituent parts, however simple or complex they may be, have made quite a coherent, efficient, satisfied creature as it relates to itself. It makes me think about the frustrations we feel in ourselves and how they feel like dissonance. What you think of yourself, what you feel, how you act and interpret yourself, where do these meet without conflict and grievance? What common ground can your parts agree on? And when they do, isn't it like music?"

"Are you saying I should know myself?"

"No, that's not how I would ask it. I mean how you would build a tenable relationship to yourself. Who you are would take too long to identify and it would bore you. You just need to find enough harmony to be happy. Finding the whole truth of any matter is immaterial because everything is ever-changing, so truth is senescent. You are not a static being; you exist in time and dilute in the world as it happens to you. You just need to be practical and find enough truth and harmony for satisfaction. I don't think it's easy but listen to me. We are very similar, so I am speaking to you from your future, like hindsight before time."

She was more serious now. The booze had made her melancholic, her eyes hardened, and she looked into her glass.

"Do you remember Malcolm's funeral? Your father gave a very good speech and I'm sure

51

that's what Malcolm would have wanted: to be remembered for his upbeat personality. There were so many people there who knew him from different corners of his life, but no-one from his home. Inside, he was very alone. I don't just mean that he never married, I mean that's the reason I believe he never married. I never found out what preyed on him so. But I think his music, when he heard his own echo, was very unhappy. I don't know the reason with any certainty but wherever he went, he tried to stop that music from leaking out, and that was very noble of him, although it would have done him some good to open up, perhaps we could have helped him. But you see all those people, including your father, came out and proclaimed what a happy, vivacious man he was. He was only ever those things as an act. I imagine he had a sad hum, but quite loud, because it invaded his life and held him back. But then there were many light parts too... I liked it very much. It was a rhythm that I did not see such and end for."

This was her way of describing the things she found painful. She didn't want to discuss this in herself, or to tell me about what else had happened in Hong Kong, or how she had been cooped up in that house for so many years alone, so she talked about herself vicariously. She was very alone and rarely left home. Whenever she did, her body now bent, and she was intimidated. She always asked me to do her shopping. Perhaps I was the only one she even told these theories of hers; I didn't know of anyone else visiting regularly.

"Everyone has grievances, Vera," I said, inviting her to speak more candidly. She avoided my eyes. Had she looked at me it would have been more difficult for her to avoid the subject, because it filled the air between us. Meeting her gaze would have forced her to speak. She pretended to misunderstand.

"You're not soft, I like that. I know everyone does, it wasn't only you included in that observation. I mean what I said."

She smiled to pretend control. It might have fooled someone else. I remembered contorting my face a million ways to avoid crying when I was a child and embarrassed to cry. Hers was the same cracked smile.

"I mean what I said, dear. Your substance and your manifestation, where do they meet and where do they split? Maybe your instruments are too complicated. Maybe there is a full orchestra that you'll have to tune."

I was flattered, but I often felt she said such things as much for her benefit as mine. It suited her music, if I should call it that, to have a protégé to take after herself. She liked it, as did I, so we kept this undercurrent in our discussions. Maybe there was something attractively complicated to unravel in me. That would have been nice to believe, but I felt derivative. I was a composite of her, and my parents, and a miscellany of stuff like everyone else. What music, what harmony? Two drum kits and a triangle I thought, and smiled wickedly, nastily about myself. Vera saw it.

"You don't have to take me seriously, but don't be conniving. Stop that." She leapt at the chance for indignance. It severed that moment of vulnerability. "Perhaps it is all a romantic idea I conjure up because the world is so unromantic. It never was what I wanted it to be. Maybe poor Pater's adulation of arts was nothing more than escapism. The greatest fluxes of vigour are organic. Love and sex are such important, earthly powers. Their heights are transcendent. And there isn't anything to transcend to, but the emotion is the same, whether the mind accurately or inaccurately perceives its significance. Poor Pater was denied that in life, so he had to find some durable substitute in art and imbued it with his needs. For all their chatter, maybe Wilhelm and Pater were just the frustrated epigones of men more animal."

That night, we dragged ourselves upstairs, slow and drunk. Vera went first while I cleaned our plates. As I walked up the stairs, I saw her through the crack in her door. She was undressing and her shape became clear for the first time. She had a spindly, spidery appearance: a potbelly and thin arms with skin hanging low from the bone. Beer swells the body and makes it fat and unwieldy, but spirits steal the same vigour in a subtler way. I understood the wisdom of her flowing clothes then.

6

To regard all things and principles of things as inconstant modes or fashions has more and more become the tendency of modern thought. Let us begin with that which is without — our physical life. Fix upon it in one of its more exquisite intervals, the moment, for instance, of delicious recoil from the flood of water in summer heat. What is the whole physical life in that moment but a combination of natural elements to which science gives their names? But those elements, phosphorus and lime and delicate fibres, are present not in the human body alone: we detect them in places most remote from it. Our physical life is a perpetual motion of them — the passage of the blood, the waste and repairing of the lenses of the eye, the modification of the tissues of the brain under every ray of light and sound — processes which science reduces to simpler and more elementary forces. Like the elements of which we are composed, the action of these forces extends beyond us: it rusts iron and ripens corn. Far out on every side of us those elements are broadcast, driven in many currents; and birth and gesture and death and the springing of violets from the grave are but a few out of ten thousand resultant combinations. That clear, perpetual outline of face and limb is but an image of ours, under which we group them — a design in a web, the

actual threads of which pass out beyond it. This
at least of flamelike our life has, that it is but the
concurrence, renewed from moment to moment,
of forces parting sooner or later on their ways.

I read through Pater's thoughts with great interest. I was indolent in that time, two months after
my first meeting with Rufus. In the beginning, I
was keen to appear keen, so that whatever mistakes I made would be forgiven, but as my familiarity with Rufus and his systems grew, so did my
security, because Rufus would not want to find
anyone else if he didn't have to and he knew Vera
and I, which counted for a lot. I became slovenly
and distracted from my little duties.

When I finished the book, I was dispirited.
Pater's descriptions of high-minded, spirited,
complete, purposeful men shone a light on my
weariness, waking up bored to my days before
they happened to me, and a chewing feeling at
the back of my mind.

The thought of 'Fitzcarraldo' and Wilhelm
Steinmetz's story came to me increasingly. I
searched through his works online and found the
unfinished picture he had described in his article.
My first impression was that it was ugly, before
the shapes became clearer and, as I followed with
increasing interest the different engagements of
its figures, it became a scene of violence. Near
the fire, clothed men hammered and worked on
the ship. The light beamed through the trees, but
most of it was lost in the thick brush, outlined by

black ridges in the paint. In the forest, the figures stopped having wholly human forms. Few men and women were wholly assembled, the other figures were concealed, except for an arm, a leg, or teeth and these grew steadily more grotesque towards the ends of the picture. Over the following days, I came back to the painting several times and it disgruntled me. Opposite the inventiveness of this piece, I was flaccid-brained and encumbered, strangled by long inert days on my bottom. The summer was over, lots of my family were dead and I was professionally immobile.

Impatience, fear and anxiety were resident in me, like everyone, but now they became too acute to ignore. I knew it by the feeling of pins and needles in my shoulders, heat under the collar and the repeating image of my brain ballooning uncomfortably. Even in the empty gallery I became stifled, sensing the displeasure of my loneliness and the exhaustion of company whenever I left.

Of all things, it was the memory of my grandfather's cat which best articulated this trouble.

He was a black cat called Vincent, come into my grandfather's possession as a kitten in a box. When he was small, he was happy to accept food and water and to be stroked lightly, but he resisted attempts to be picked up and manhandled, as I learned when he bit quite deep into my index finger with his fine porcelain teeth. Blood came out and I cried and hated him for a while

57

but eventually I forgave him after he jumped on the couch and padded across me gracefully to dig himself in under my arm. He forgave me, and I decided not to stickle with him either.

Vincent was my grandfather's companion for long years after my grandmother died. First, he was independent and sprightly like other cats. His freedom was all he valued, and he protested too much stroking and fought back when I put my foot under his belly to make him walk like a wheelbarrow. He was his own cat and our presence in his life was secondary to his life outside.

This changed as he got older and fatter and sought ways to countervail his diminishing self-sufficiency. Vincent slowly became more playful. He walked between my grandfather's legs and trailed his tail; he sat and watched him as he cooked, hopped on a chair as he ate and demanded affection and to be lifted. If these were not effective at melting the heart, he meowed softly, then louder if he was ignored. My grandfather was helpless, and Vincent grew much fatter as his portions and their frequency increased. He did not go outside as much; in fact, after a long meal he and my grandfather would usually have a little sleep together on the sofa. I thought this was the most wonderful thing because of the way he had evolved.

My grandfather was a god in Vincent's life. The cat food he ate, the underarm he liked to curl under to sleep, the door to his home, were all controlled by this one towering figure of unfathomable motivations. But Vincent pulled himself out of the dark. By some calculation, he found how to influence his god. Meowing and stroking, he prayed to be lent an ear and to have fortune showered on himself, and he was successful. Their relationship grew in complexity and my grandfather once swore that Vincent had different meowing sounds when they said hello to each other in the morning, when he wanted to get food, and when he wanted to get picked up.

There was some part of him that had grown in awareness and intellectual versatility, because he meowed to me as well, recognizing a being like my grandfather, with some sway over his fate. He walked through my legs as well and begged me for food, though he was quite sure which god had the most influence and always solicited my grandfather before all others. He valued their bond, so he became a very sociable animal.

The most wonderful thing about Vincent's transformation was that he was right. He curried favour with a life force whose usefulness he guessed, then played upon. So, for a cat, he had undergone an Enlightenment, when the bounds of cat-life changed from a being that fended for itself, to an interpersonal, social creature, aware of its place in a chain, and cunning enough to achieve its ends therein.

As a child, sitting with Vincent on my lap, looking me in the eye, I was impressed by his achievements, because Vincent had the peace and satisfactions of a devout, religious man. Now

I wondered if I would ever have such a revelation because, next to the majestic ascent of that cat, I, Profligate Wastrel, was a Dark Age man, plodding up icy stairs in oily flippers.

7

Whatever I thought, soon forces outside the influence of my efforts worked on me.

In *Paradise Lost*, John Milton describes the construction of Pandemonium, the palace of demon-kind after they have tumbled out of heaven. The infernal headquarters are built in a flourish by legions of demons. They are majestic and woeful but also very small, small enough that the demons must shrink themselves down to get inside.

This miscellany came to me one night and I imagined a red figure, with a goat's head and horns, sticking its head out of my ear. That night was the birthday of a close friend of mine. After drinking quite a lot at his house in the day, we had gone to a pub nearby, where the birthday boy convinced me to slow down because I was too drunk. That came after a lot of shouting and spilling most of my pint over the floor and trying to mop it up with the sole of my shoe. I became sullen and quiet, embarrassed and unwilling to speak. As I waited to sober up and for the urge to speak to return (it would not), I pondered the parliament of demons to pass the time, watching the others enjoy themselves. When they all decided to go to a club, which I had no interest or money for, I made an excuse and left the party. On the way home, I tried to think of the names of the individual figures in the *Infernal Dictionary* and the *Lesser Key of Solomon* and the moods they were supposed to govern. It would have seemed grand to find an old, demonic figure that created apathy, misanthropy, weak will and drunken party fowls, or however those categorizations work. Looking back now, I think I got it wrong: I had meant to think about William Blake more than Milton, but I would have been too drunk to look it up either way.

When I got home, I was bitter to discover that I had lost my keys. There was no answer when I rang the bell, and I remembered my parents would be gone for the weekend. The options I could see were to return to the pub that was surely closed and beg to scrabble around for the keys, wait for whenever my parents returned, or sleep on the sofa in the coffee room above the gallery a little walk away. I decided on the last option and set off angrily. I bought food on the way to sober myself up and thought up what I would watch as I ate my food once I got there. I arrived, punched in the code to retrieve the key from the box and let myself in.

I took off most of my clothing before eating so that I would be most comfortable and sat down on the felt couch to my can of coke, battered chicken and chips. I put my headphones in and watched the gameplay for a video game that would be coming out the following year. When I had finished eating, it occurred to me that I should put the empty box of fried food outside this room; otherwise the smell would be more difficult to air out in the morning. I got up again and opened the door only to find Rufus on the landing, accompanied by his sloanie old girl. They looked at me (in my pants) incredulously. I tried to think up the beginnings of an explanation, starting by removing the earbuds that blared machine gun and monster sounds. I mumbled something, but it was obviously useless. Rufus smiled and laughed (I think to preserve the good spirits of his companion) and said "it's always like this" as if we were two charming, mad people who were always up to these sorts of antics. I explained what had happened to me and they both nodded knowingly, and she said, "these things happen", but Rufus told me they were hoping to have a drink in the room, so I said I was going to leave anyway, it was no trouble. Rufus said he'd see me out and he truly did, firing me the minute we crossed the threshold of the gallery.

As I waited for the morning and my parents' return, I felt a cavernous disappointment growing in my chest. I was weary and jobless. I told myself I needed system shock and defibrillation so that I could adjust the course of my person. I still think that was a perceptive conclusion, even if I couldn't trace the origin of the problem. With hours to spare till daybreak, I let myself dream of magical places I could go, as Wilhelm, Herzog and Vera had before me. It was that slow trickle of thoughts that would soon lead me abroad, then to the *Relais*.

8

The week before my departure, I stayed with Vera again. She had been complaining about her health and asked me to help around the house and in the kitchen. It was a cold, overcast day. I was woken by the cold in my feet and tucked them under my blankets. I could see my breath and frost flowers on the window pane that looked over the road.

I made tea and cooked us some breakfast and when we'd finished, we went for a constitutional walk. But it was a very dry; cold and moisture had crystalized in the mud, making it glitter and difficult to walk over, so we turned back early and walked back in silence.

My plans had been made clandestinely, away from her though we shared everything during that time. I found myself very unwilling to speak to her about leaving, a subject sure to upset and disappoint her. That was the opinion of my parents as well, though they had taken the news with matter-of-fact ease. Even as I explained myself, my mother had come around and tousled my hair to calm me as I tripped over my sentences, struggling to explain my decision and referring, without context, to what I had learned from Vera, Pater and Steinmetz and my expanding balloon. Across the table, my father had rubbed his chin in thought and surprised me when he said "Good idea. Variety is the spice of life after all and it will probably do you some good to get a change of air. Wouldn't it, my dear?" My mother nodded. They were more surprised when I explained my intention to leave before Christmas, but I was insistent on the urgency of departure. Later my mother would call my decision a 'common growth pain' and my father would call it an osteotomy. They were understanding but this youthful thrashing and confusion was perfectly ordinary and no real cause for concern to them, though it felt that way to me.

Vera would not see it that way; she would think of herself, as I was then, seeing her take off her coat with difficulty and weakly wiping her boots on the doormat. I realized I would have to say it that day. Keeping the news would be more incriminating. She looked me in the eye.

"What's wrong?"

"Nothing," I lied with a warm smile.

We sat in silence and read, but after only a short while she clapped her magazine closed and grinned, staring blankly ahead of her.

"Do you know what I would like to do?" she asked. I shook my head. "I would like to spend the day together in the studio, like when you were little. Do you remember?" I nodded. "Well? Go on, what do you think?"

The thought of resuscitating this childhood memory ahead of my revelation bolstered my anxiety. She saw me wavering.

"I told you what a hell I've been through this week. I hate, hate, hate going to the hospital because it just takes it all out of me. But I feel much better now, and I want to paint again. We can make it like before. I'll put on some music, we can make a big pot of tea and empty the biscuit tin and just paint whatever we feel like all day."

I feared opening that door, but I had not yet mustered the courage to tell her why. I said yes and she got up like a spring. She put the kettle on and started looking through her CDs, whistling and shaking her hips from side to side like a younger person. She chose *Pet Sounds* and encouraged me to sing as I had when I was a boy. I tried to reach the high notes again, but it was more difficult.

When the tea and biscuits were potted and plated, we went into her studio. I hadn't been in there for many years, but she had a canvas already set up on her easel. It was brighter than most of the other pieces lying about the place. In the centre she had drawn the outlines of a shape that was spitted over a fire. Looking closer, I found it was a human figure and bound to the spit with rings over the whole body. Around this central motif, she had already drawn and filled in a black circle and around that the outline of a crossed window through which could be seen another unfinished human. I looked down to the end of the garden and the neighbours' house over the hedge.

I sat down and nibbled a biscuit, looking at the old paintings I had almost forgotten about. Vera saw me and smiled with girlish sweetness like I hadn't seen in years. She loosened her hair and turned her attention to her canvas, muttering assurances to herself. She froze in contemplation for a few minutes then started scratching away at the canvas with her pencil. I picked a sketch pad up from the floor hopelessly and tried to press some idea out of my brain.

At midday, she offered me a glass of wine. I said I wasn't feeling well, but she convinced me I'd be fine. If she was drinking in her condition, a strapping, young man like me could certainly have a glass. She poured them out and we brought our glasses together gingerly. She confessed she had not been able to find me another job and apologized. I told her not to be sorry.

I couldn't think of a way to tell her; I couldn't think of the first words that would open the floodgate. I wanted her to suss it out of me alone, but on that day she was too caught up in her fantasy. Under normal circumstances, we knew each other too well for her not to guess a feeling in me. If I spoke too eagerly, it would betray a desire to let it out and an admission of guilt. If I spoke slowly, however, if I looked left and right as if confused, and avoided her eyes at times, but kept a serious face, like one in difficult contemplation, then perhaps, when the truth came out, she would feel sorry for me and be grateful that she meant enough to me to put me in turmoil. I wanted her to feel things in me which I didn't know how to say. But there was a shameful trickery there and I emphasized my own pain by staring at the ground for long periods, hoping she would turn around and see it. I wanted to incur sympathy for a decision that, really, had caused me only delight. I felt guilty and it finally struck me what it would mean to be separated from Vera again, especially now that I was one of her few remaining joys.

Late in the afternoon when it was already dark outside and colder in our room, Vera put her brush close to the canvas and hesitated, the bristles hovering millimetres from the surface. Seeing her freeze, I raised my eyes to her and the canvas. She had made some progress. A first layer of colour had been painted over the humanoids and there was more detailing in the window and on the rings and she had faded out the black a bit so that the edges were no longer sharp. She took a few steps and let her hand fell to her side with a puzzled expression. She was out of breath as she spoke.

"Do you know... I hate this piece. I do, I do, I hate it." I bit my lip as she spoke. I always liked what she painted. Vera's face sharpened, her eyes narrowed, and she touched her thumb to each of her fingers in succession. "I'm going to put my foot through it." And with that she took it down from the easel and before I could say anything, she had stamped on the canvas.

She went out for a minute and came back with the wine bottle. She poured herself a glass and drank it in one draught, then her face relaxed with relief and pleasure. I had seen her do this once before, as a child. She had had an argument on the phone and hung up violently. I was waiting in the doorway, but she didn't see me. Out of the cupboard, I saw her take a bottle of whiskey and take a swig. Her shoulders quivered then relaxed. She checked her breath against her hand then she took an apple from the fridge and took a bite. I crept back to the living room quietly. When she came back in my parents asked her what happened, and she said it was no matter.

"There is something much worse happening in that house than I could articulate," she said and held her head high and proud again. "There's somewhere in me that always feels like I cheapen the world when I paint. It's like those songs about love that speak only in broad strokes. The night, the beauty, dancing, wine and delight. It is primitive and misleading to misrepresent the world and put it in such childish terms. I'm glad I put my foot through that awful piece because it was hollow. I wanted to make something fashionable and... well, how childish and low."

She looked down at her feet, still holding her

glass. She looked at me for an answer, but I could only watch. She had built herself up to a great height as she spoke. Her expression turned in an instant and she came to my side. She was soft and knelt down, pushing her face closer to mine and taking my hand.

"What is it, my darling?" she asked, seeing my act.

I can't say why, but in that moment, I realized that I had never asked Vera what any of those people in the ground had been to her. I knew the family tree, but what she thought of them, and how she missed them, I never asked. I had thought it better to keep her from such thoughts, but she perhaps thought of nothing else when I left. I had made provisions only to keep myself happy, drinking and listening to her past and never once trying to comfort her for her inevitable future. And if not me, I couldn't see who would help her because she could not admit her own fragility.

Even now as she was creaking open, she was coming to help me. She was soft in that instance, but she could turn so quickly again, returning up her proud tower. I would have liked to tell her what I thought of her, but it would be unwieldy. I wanted to ask how she could think so little of herself, when she was so much to me. Had I spoken, the air we shared would have disintegrated. To be pitied by me would set her on fire. I mumbled some words of explanation and said I was sorry to leave her at that time, because I knew how close we had become, but she didn't let me finish. She got up again and looked down squarely. When I said I would call her, she left the room.

Limbo followed. For a time, I discontinued the physical centre of my life, which was home and the main dramatis personae near me, to seek isolation, regeneration and a bit of oblivion of my own.

9

My destination came to me through John Cale's 1973 album, *Paris 1919*. On the cover, Mr. Cale wears a white suit in a small sepia window against an otherwise white cover. It is a chic and understated picture. The eponymous song to the album is a favourite of mine, and following it comes a song about Graham Greene. When I looked up Graham Greene, I found that he had written *The Quiet American*, where the hero is a British man in Saigon. From this association, a series of fantasies flowered which showed me sitting in ease, looking out over a lustrous city in the sun, my blood refreshed like Vera's and Wilhelm's had been. On the morning of my departure, my father gave me his copy of the book, saying "I'm sure the place has changed a lot, but it's a good book" and my mother gave me navy swimming trunks with a pattern of Quentin Blake-ish bananas. I was already half-disappeared before I reached the airport. From my seat at the window, I saw the colours of the houses, fields and roads dilute to each other, then new bright ones appear.

Saigon is coloured for the sun. Its makeup is soft old white, cream, yellow and blanched pastels that blend into one another. The colours catch the light when it shines and sink into the sky when it doesn't. At its highest point in the dry season, the glare may completely repaint the city, and then it glows from a gilt of copper sunlight. In those moments, all who can will go indoors or sit in the shade because the heat bastes the skin.

It is more intimate than a European city. People sleep in public, or on their scooters, food is eaten on the side of the road, at little plastic or aluminium tables and strangers speak to each other quite freely, so one could walk, sit, sell, sleep, eat or drink on any pavement without causing disturbance.

On the roads, drivers flood forward, pushing out in eddies when a gap presents itself, and shrinking back when it closes, and new gaps open. Cars are less frequent and block up the narrow streets and alleys which they cross. Scooters follow behind them like pilot fish, shielded from oncoming traffic. There is a frequent din and honking, and the petrol of so many engines can accumulate like the hot vapor of burned spirits in your throat.

In the outer districts the buildings are built to

71

random heights, and little towers poke out of the alleys that spiderweb between the main roads. These are filled with life and bustle. There are always cafes, always shops for bits-and-bobs and always places for food. The city feeds people like kings.

I stayed in a hostel to start with. I was in a simple room with lacquered nightstands over which were laid stickers that looked like fine wood. I had chosen to be near the backpacker street, a place of some renown for being a drunken wilderness which I thought would suit me.

So much false good and evil is said about the effect of alcohol that perhaps it is impossible to find any truth about it, other than whether one likes or dislikes the sensation of drunkenness. That, most people can answer quite clearly. My own relationship to it has changed dramatically. As a child it was promising and frightening. Being forbidden, like too much TV or too many sweets, signified it was good until I got to taste it, in so many forms. Then I would pull a face, because it was nothing like I had expected and never very close to Coca-Cola or lemonade, which were the best drinks, so good that I didn't really see why we had punished ourselves by not having them at every meal. When I got to the age to start dabbling in alcohol away from parents, I was apprehensive. I looked very young for a very long time, only climbing up to my gangly stature around 17, and facial hair only sprouting a few years later. It was a problem to be served alcohol, and to avoid the embarrassment of being thrown out of a pub along with my friends, and the fear of being a liability, made me take on puritanical views about the booze. I told myself it was infantile and that, like my parents, I should act with restraint. My father had the same views, and once when I was 13 explained to me all the ways alcohol had negatively affected his friends. He pointed out the dangers of drunkenness in the short and long term and the ripple effects of its abuse. His sage views became mine, right until I got a fake ID and decided I would risk these perils to impress girls and friends. Then the fear left, and I became enthusiastic about the stuff, like everyone else, hiding in faraway bits of the school grounds to smoke and drink. The image of it is ridiculous because we made such an effort to drink, where it is now an effortless side effect. It was impressive and grown up, and when we had beer it was all we wanted. We could drink anywhere without ever asking what else we could be doing. Drinking was the activity we came for and it was wholly satisfying. In the holidays I would siphon leftover money from around the house for nights trying our luck at successive pubs and then let the one friend who got served buy all the drinks, so that no-one else had to run the risk of ruining the night. And if the bar staff looked over suspiciously, we leaned back and acted unfussed with our drinks to persuade them of our maturity. But really there was a lot of fuss, and there was no greater feeling than coming back to your table with beer or coming out of an off-license with booze and seeing the glowing look of your friends and girls who you didn't know what might happen with. The excitement cured me of my faux-maturity, and we all came to like it. We drank badly, as kids do, but even throwing up and other accompanying disgraces drunkenness brought could do little to hamper how badly we wanted to drink. At first, we drank for each other and status, and then we started to drink more for our own pleasure. We were still so far from realizing its perils, so we went swimming.

I'm still impressed by the masculinity of leather-faced booze-hounds, and Vera's, of course, my queen of booze-hounds, and the fact that they cannot help their drinking has endeared me to some people as I see some unfair force acting on them and see them wishing to forget and be left alone, preferably oblivious. It deserves pity, though of course there are devilish, cruel drunkards. I was an embarrassing drunk (I still am) and pushed myself to extremes because it seemed like a cool thing to do (it still does). I liked to think it made me devil-may-care-ish and confident, which will always be attractive. But really, I just enjoy being drunk and that's all there is to it. To avoid that unattractive reflection, I have always found reasons to romanticize the process of drinking and, thereby, my own drinking. I never had many masculine qualities, having been a weak sportsman like my father, uninterested in watching sport, unable to discuss politics, beardless, shy, reserved, prone to melancholy and over-sentimentality, so I welcomed opportunities I had to upend this personality. I took inspiration from great drinkers like Oliver Reed and Gerry Rafferty, who balanced this animal that is so important, particularly in youth, with a higher spirit, something misunderstood and complex that fought in public, but earned a quiet respect in private. This slow burn brand of drinker, one who is serious, whose physical and mental ferocity is chained but potent, is how I tried to cast myself. Those men had loneliness to cure, like Malcolm I imagine, but they found very different solutions. When I didn't treat alcohol with such severity (the quality in me that too often crystalizes when drunk and makes me so embarrassing), I found reasons to celebrate it. To make the drunkenness seem more noble, I idolized a passage about alcohol from Washington Irving, an American who described an old Christmas in England in the early 19th Century. The pater familias, a blue-blooded country gentleman who lives with his family in a sodden old country estate, is the primary subject of the author. I imagined him as a bulbous, gouty, wizened bigot. Irving wrote that the man complained about the modern fashion of drinking tea and coffee in the morning, and said he preferred fortified wine and meat for his breakfast. It left a big impression in me for the very hunterly, bloody, gothic feeling and the cold of his big hall. I could almost taste the red meat and fancied myself as someone of the same ilk, because I might not refuse a drink at breakfast if someone would drink with me.

Luckily, I had recovered somewhat from these ideas about alcohol over my death-summer and renewed proximity with Vera, but my wisdom was dashed upon arrival in the wilderness. The abundance of neon, loud music, cheap alcohol and the grotesque, ribald vibrations took me up gladly.

"Oooooohhhhhhhh it was sooo spiritual! You have no idea. Have you ever been to the North? We met this family and they let us stay there for a while and cut the prices of the room and we developed this real bond, like, they'd let us watch their baby and then at night we'd just smoke and drink beer and palm wine. It was so peaceful, such a great experience. We're thinking of moving there."

This story came from an Australian girl with a shrill voice, like two sheets of metal scraping together. We listened and nodded, and her boyfriend kept smoking, smiling with agonising idiocy.

"But of course, we had to go. You know, the long road of life, you have to travel it and you make great friends on the way and you enrich each other."

She looked devastatingly earnest as she spoke.

"D'you remember babe? And like by the end we were speaking every day even though they didn't speak English. We just got it, you know what I mean? You can just learn the language that way."

"You speak Vietnamese?" Asked a guy we were with, "How long were you there?"

"Only a week but you know I read a bit and I'm very intuitive and we just had that feeling you know what I mean?"

"We laughed every day," said the boyfriend, "remember when we told him what 'we're not here to fuck spiders' means? Remember babe?"

"Oh yeeeee, ooooooohhh sooo lush. He was like duh-duh-duh-ching-chong something in Vietnamese and we laughed so much."

The boyfriend leaned over and did the finger-in-the-hole gesture and then moved his hand up her arm like a spider.

"That's how we told him!"

Such was the character of my first days. We gathered in our pinfold and drank, and I heard about adventures from across the world, many involving, at some point, the words 'we were so drunk' and 'I had to go to the hospital'. I don't think anyone ever made the connection, but as we battered and bruised, optimistic foreigners huddled together in tourist bars, there was a palpable sense of self-contentment. We had all escaped the humdrumness of everyday life where we were from, we were adventurers and we enjoyed our liberty in bottles, cans, cigarettes, and cheap, rubbish drugs.

I was surprised to find how easily we all became friends. I could join in, especially when people made fun of my accent and said, 'you British are so and so...'. I had opinions about football, which I had never had or considered before, I made jokes about the Queen and tea and I called an American a Yank, and a French girl called me a *ros'beef* and we all chuckled at our charming, guarded internationalism

It didn't feel so very far from home. In the first week, I spoke to a very tall man with a paunch and six years of solid teaching experience under his belt who befriended me quickly on account of our both being English. He said he had moved because everything at home was getting too samey, and nothing changed. The man who had encouraged him to move was an old friend from school. I think the man was sick and couldn't breathe through his nose as he told me the story, because he kept his mouth wide open and breathed out a heavy draught of beer. His pronunciation was mottled with saliva. It was like two wet gammon steaks slapping together, or a lisping platypus.

"His name was Peter, but we called him Partyboy because he just wouldn't stop. You know one of those guys who one-ups anything you say or drink. I met him at university during a quiz at the student union and afterwards we went and got very drunk at the pub. It got proper mental though, let me tell you. We ended up buying a lot of vodka and other shit and had a competition who could jump off the highest balcony in our accommodations. I actually jumped off the highest one, but he broke both his ankles jumping off a lower one. Of course, he won for that, but we

had to get him to hospital. Hahahahahahahaha-
haha."

He drained his glass and laughed wholeheart-
edly.

"Anyway, Partyboy got both his legs all plastered up and the hospital offered him crutches
cos they got no wheelchairs left. He said, 'it's no
good having crutches, I can't use my feet,' but
they said like 'yea, sorry mate, got no wheelchairs.' I swear, I don't know how he got around,
he must have learned to balance himself weird or
something. But one night, we were all in this club
and we'd all had a few drinks, a couple of the lads
copped off with some girls and we all went home
but we forgot Partyboy. I think he was fucked
too. Hahahaha. So the next day we're all like 'shit
where's Partyboy, who did he come home with?'
He's a mate, so we gotta find him. But no-one
knew where he was, so I walked back to the club
and I knocked on the door. A man came out and
I told him who we were looking for, so he said
he saw him leaving around the corner at closing
time. I went around the corner and guess what I
saw? It's not Partyboy, just his crutches. He was
so pissed he couldn't use them and pulled himself
home like a seal!'

I roared with laughter.

When the hotel man saw me come home that
night, hunched and rough like a sick bird, he
laughed and said "England love beer! Drink a
lot!" I tried to explain what binge drinking was,
but the cultural phenomenon was beyond my

means to convey with hands and the conversation became awkward. I laughed it off, he kindly joined in, and we both mimed lifting barrels over our mouths, and he patted me on the back. "*Shy-sumdi, shysumdi!*" he said as I left him, and I said it back. I didn't know what he meant but when I flopped into bed that night, it was with a head still full of England.

The alley my hotel was tucked into suited me well at first, but I did not stay very long. There were people selling food, a little shop to buy Coca-Cola, cigarettes, tissues and other bits, a barber, a mechanic and a place selling fake brand shoes, which was all to my flavour except for one man: the cockfighter. He was a fat man with short, cropped hair in military fashion and he always lifted his T-shirt over his belly when it was hot, as he sat outside smoking and chatting to the others. His manners didn't bother me, but his business, and his cockerel, were a source of constant grief. The man woke up earlier than me, usually around 5, and uncovered the cock's cage at about the same time, giving him plenty of time to crow as the sun started to come up. Every morning, often fighting a hangover, I'd pull myself from my bed to the window and look across the few feet between our balconies and see this hellish animal screaming its lungs out. Clueless for a riposte, I had to start my day then or try to bury my ears under pillows and blankets to allow me a bit more sleep.

Sometimes as I left the building, I'd see the beast fighting for its life as men stood around in a circle, and I'd hope for the worst. But after more than a week this prize chicken fought and won and continued to scream me awake, red-eyed and fuming.

One day, I decided to take matters into my own hands. I walked over to the building and saw the fat owner. He spoke clear English and asked me what I wanted. I said he had to do something about the noise and he said no-one else had any complaints and he had nowhere else to put the chicken. I protested. He protested back, until eventually I offered to buy the chicken off him. What would I do with it? I didn't know. I told it I'd drive it to another district and set it loose to torture someone else, imagining all the while how I could cook and eat my enemy if I got it. We haggled for a while, but the man would go no lower than about £50 for his chicken, which felt very steep to me. In a huff, I returned home.

As his fights wore on, the chicken became more and more dishevelled. To the cockfighter's credit, he treated it well aside from making it fight. I saw him wash it and paint over its discoloured feathers to give it back its red lustre, and he stroked its crest when he picked it up.

The nightmare persisted until the inevitable day when, driving home, I saw the man plucking the headless body. He gave me a knowing smile and lifted the carcass to show me, and I smiled inside but not outside. By the time it had fought its last, I had already made my arrangements for a more permanent residence to flee him and plant my roots.

I left the hotel and took a pokey studio nearby, having grown quite accustomed to my area and the pho and rice places I frequented. It was a simple room all alone on the top floor of a fat, cosy building. The owner had taken great care to homogenize the interiors in a Japanese style. There were dark faux-wood floorboards, brown and beige furnishings and sliding squared shutters on the windows. I had the choice of either keeping the low dining table with sitting cushions or taking a high-seated chair and desk. I didn't want to impose so I accepted the little table with a smile, and became used to it in time. He and I were very good friends in broken English. However, after I had paid my first month's rent and a deposit, the urgency of money struck, and I started searching for work teaching English. I searched for work online and quickly became inundated with offers from schools and people seeking private lessons. I planned a schedule that allowed me to live comfortably, if not profitably, as I already knew with some certainty that I would not like teaching, but I required stability. Everything slid into a comfortable routine. Every morning I had cereal and coffee in my room, hopped on my scooter, and joined the city's current, pushing forward languidly as I woke up. I'd get to the school, check myself for signs of perspiration, wander up to my classroom, prepare some bits about cats and dogs and verbs and nouns and then spend a few hours correcting students.

Such was the usual, pleasant run of my middle days as they turned into weeks, and then months; I got to know the city and visited the old French buildings, the post office, Notre Dame de Saigon, the museums and the waving statue of Uncle Ho on the big plaza called Nguyen Hue. I went out to expatriate bars where the beer was more expensive, and the waiters spoke English and the TVs played American and European sports, but also smaller establishments where locals sat at tin tables with a box of beer under the table, and a bucket of ice to keep the beer cold. We packed these places with our shouting and calling, our unconcerned ordering and guffawing, and it was the youngest I had felt in a long time.

With new youth came energy and curiosity. The luxury of cities, jungles and seasides on that corner of the world was therapeutic. It was hot everywhere. Vegetation grew everywhere that hadn't been plastered with concrete, and teams of workmen sawed and cut to push it back where it crept back in, the vines climbing lampposts, the roots disfiguring streets and the brush pushing through the pavement. To confront things that are unfamiliar is the governing feeling of childhood, so it was natural to feel rejuvenated by my sudden ignorance of everything around me and the curiosity it awoke when I saw pink temples like honeyed cake in Malaysia, or the windows of the white church in Singapore where the stained glass looks like wine gums.

I was never sad to come home either. I built my nest very quickly and soon Saigon was homely, with a few exceptions:

10

It is often remarked that humour does not lend itself to translation. The quality of it depends on immediacy, which needs a speed of association that only comes with cultural familiarity. Once a joke must be explained, that feeling on a needlepoint is lost; it stretches out and its workings lose their spark as they appear deliberate and processed like a sausage, rather than a sudden, wonderful creation. There is of course humour that cannot dull, because it reflects essential sides of life. Early comedians like Charlie Chaplin and Buster Keaton have this quality, I think. Everyone will laugh at the tramp, because his movements reflect the stuff of us all. His humour has intimacy and communality, having been experienced in some form by us all. We have all caught ourselves weirdly at odds with the world. It's funny to see and gratifying to know that we all share that. We enjoy the empathy and understanding. Any explanation would ruin the charm of feeling that we understand one another just so and kill the electricity.

Comfort is hard to translate as well. At home, I knew what it was. It was the warm music with Vera, films that featured likeable, consoling stories about defeated evil, old, supernatural things in fantastical, beautiful, caring worlds, it was Christmas, cake, family, tea and warmth against the cold. Of these, food was perhaps the only thing I could take comfort in whenever I was melancholic. There was no precise object of melancholy, but only that solution, more universal even than humour. My only other attempt came from reading my books, but it wasn't right. After Greene, I found nothing else I could read. I had taken *Idylls of the King* with me, but Tennyson, fields, swords and knights had no place in my head, when all around me was an atmosphere so alien to them. Through the windows were palm trees, oven heat, a language I didn't understand, and little trace of what I knew. Such disjointed feelings were distracting and so I found little except food to reconstitute the feeling of safety and care of consolation until I met a real friend.

It was on my street that I met Julian. We met in a supermarket queue and discussed the overuse of plastic to pass the time before passing onto something meaningful. When I asked him where he was from he said "Oh me? I'm from a small town in southern California that you'd recognize instantly by its iconic strip mall, best-in-class burger bars, pizza places and fast-food chains. It's the suburban, nothing-to-worry-about dream with year-round sunshine and a low chance of feeling disillusioned."

He was self-effacing, speckled with little insecurities and darting, evasive eyes. He was half-Vietnamese, tall with soft, thin black hair, a thin build that evidently only rounded out with weight as he reached his late 20s and early 30s, a slim but full, cheeky face, thin arms and legs and a dark, burnished eye colour in wide, not very deep sockets. When I asked him how long he'd been in the country, he withdrew his cigarette and said "too long" with a wry, sheepish smile. We went for a drink soon after, and I saw that he liked to drink quite considerably as well. He was very polite with the waiters, and only ever spoke to them in Vietnamese, though by his own admission the pronunciation gave him great trouble. We spoke about films, and science-fiction, but he only eased up late, when he was already drunk. Then his movements became more fluid, he stopped tugging his nose and mouth so often, and he spoke more steadily. I was evidently more at ease than him, but he guessed I was impressed by the fact that he was more at home there than me. He said he had come over to escape the monotony, and to connect with family. He'd gone to the north to see them, but it hadn't worked out, and he came back to Ho Chi Minh City. Though wiry, he could be forceful. A handful of times he referred to the "bad expats" who exploited their status; I wasn't sure if he included me among them but he listed his pet hatreds, all of which involved those people who never joined this world, but remained in the luxurious bubble they were given without effort. I hoped he did not count me among them, but I made mistakes. A few weeks after we'd met, I remember haggling for a trinket to send my parents at home. He brusquely told me to stop, took the money out of my hands and gave it to the vendor and led us away, steaming and embarrassed by me.

"What are you haggling with that man for?" he asked angrily. "He has so much less than you, what do you care about two dollars?" I said I didn't want to be cheated. "So, you don't want to look like a dope? Screw your pride and don't be so selfish. Have some decency."

I was fond of him after that. He was quiet and became more openly irascible as we got to know each other. I tried to introduce him to my wilderness friends, but he left us after the first drink and told me he didn't want to know more people like that. But we two got along fine, bonding over our books and films, our mutual interest in boozing and the fact that his manners and outbursts never offended me, like it did most of the people he used to know.

We met regularly enough to convince me I was his only friend. Sometimes we drank and played PlayStation at his flat. It was a small ruin in the first district of the city. The building had leprous exteriors and a pile-up of rubbish in the courtyard that was emptied irregularly. The walls inside were not much better, although the managers had bothered to cover the craters where the cement had fallen out.

Through mindless fun-seeking, my expatriation became a period outside of regular time. It was Julian who brought me back with a simple question, more serious than any I had asked in a while: 'why are you here?' It made me defensive. I felt my blood rush and the brief white panic of having my shame discovered. I flung about for a reason of substance that would explain me to him in a way that would increase, or at least maintain his esteem for me, and mine for myself. But all I found was something far tawdrier. 'To find myself' I answered, truthfully, flatly. I felt my music jar and immediately wished I had lied, but at the time of that question I was also hungover, and lacking wherewithal. I had to persevere with an explanation.

"It is not as stupid as it sounds." For my ego's sake I had to believe that I was a cut above the nonsense people who said the same, illustrating their ambition for self-discovery with a syncretic spirituality. "I don't mean it in that shallow way."

"It's too commonplace for you? You snob. What confluence of miracles made you so special?" Julian was too straightforward for me that day. I easily forgave the light indiscretions of his rudeness, most of which could not even touch me, but this was painful to tolerate, as close as it was to my Adam, which had, since my arrival, become more fragile.

For that wound Julian gave me, I followed him closely thereafter. He was the only person who had reached me since my arrival; the only person of consequence who would tie me back to my centre and to Vera, who never could leave me fully in that period of my life. In fact, he recalled her to me quite by accident.

We had gone to Da Lat, a small city in the highlands. It was built by the French and used as a place of respite during the First Indochinese War. Its temperate climes were as welcome a relief from the heat of Saigon back then as they were for Julian and me. We took an overnight bus into the city and spent the morning walking about to take in the unique blend of Vietnamese and Alpine architectures that made that town distinct. We spoke about this curio at length, and the distance it made us feel from the rest of the country, whose heat and noise were the primary characteristics. By the time we had arrived at the house of the last emperor, Bao Dai, Julian was explaining a quandary to me.

"The problem was to try and find a practical way to mix the two different mentalities," he said as we walked. We were in the garden then, marching among pine trees and faint classical music that played through small hidden speakers. These distracted me until Julian pulled my attention back to himself indignantly. "Do you know what I'm saying?" he inquired, and I nodded yes. "Right. The French system in all its intricacies was incongruous on so many fronts with local suppositions about the world. The most widespread social customs came from Confucianism and it's the Confucian structure which defined most social norms. That still brings out the differences between people here and you and I, the *người nước ngoại.*'

I nodded with a little interest. Julian peppered his speech with Vietnamese terminology which gave us both a sense of proximity to the land.

'That system, which came from China, emphasized so many different ideas from the ones the French brought over. Confucianism emphasizes the many ways a person fits into social structures, from a family, to a village, to a nation. I think that's why it merges with Buddhism: the cyclicality of it, the way it teaches that we are not independent individuals, but bonded individuals, feels like an ideological overlap between both. Point is that people in this society always believed and had ingrained in them that they belonged to a structure with others. There was an ontological, indivisible link between one person and their family, society, and so on. It was everywhere, this feeling, and there's even a concept here that children owe their parents an unpayable debt for the gift of their lives. That's not like us, is it? We exist much more in isolation. The Declaration of the Rights of Man, that holiest French document, focused on individualism and what is inalienable from a person regardless of any affiliation. I'm not saying that's bad, but the mentality that is consequent to that hotpot of ideas has many conflicts here, where it was championed by a conquering people. The individualism from that declaration set off a chain reaction of thoughts centred on what the individual is, and the value of the independent individual. But that delineation, that amputation of one person from another, was not in the common imagination of this world before the West arrived.'

We kept walking and entered the house of the last emperor. It had red carpeting and warm, glowing lights which reminded me of *The Grand Budapest Hotel* in colouration. The walls were lined with old photographs from the colonial era, at which we lingered with great interest. Maybe two hundred tourists, mostly Chinese, were there with us and I had to take a break from our discussion as I was corralled into photos. I looked funny, big, ungainly and bedraggled. For a while, I had enjoyed the distinction of my ethnicity and taken its advantages with a smile. But this late it annoyed me. I wished to pass without remark, so I was relieved when Julian gestured quite forcefully that we had to leave, making that excuse for me. We went upstairs, and he continued.

'There's maybe nowhere that this French corruption is more obvious than here. We're in the house of the last emperor, a man who was considered by his people to be a colonial puppet, and we've already talked about the strange mix of architectural styles. But a mentality has much bigger scale, and the French brought that. What would it feel like, you know? To be suddenly ruled by a group of people who have little interest in adopting your beliefs, only replacing them? The ideas of the individual bound only to themselves, that pioneer mould, that capitalist, that American person who values their own freedoms against all aggressors, physical and spiritual; they see that person on TV... Ideas are slow but dogged in their advances. You could argue that Catholicism was a big spiritual revolution here, but society has a spirituality to it as well, even when it is dissociated from religion. It's a structure of ideas, feelings and interest in each other. The tenets of a society are its interpretation of what is meaningful and valuable in the world.'

'Then what happened with the French ideas here?' I asked. 'Where did the ideas go?'

'Well... They're still here. The colonies are gone in name, but their economic and philosophical weight is still felt. Nowadays it's more American power, but that's largely a descendant of European, specifically French ideas. And young people here care less and less about their place in the old chain of existence that they used to believe in; more people want to seize their individuality. It's what they see other, mostly richer people doing on TV and talking about in their songs. Kids want more and more freedom from their parents, and increasingly it's moving that way.'

'Isn't that a good thing though? We should all have the power to decide for ourselves who we will be. I mean... most of the stories you see here are Romeo and Juliet. They're all about love gone wrong because the parents don't allow it to happen. All the stories are about dissatisfaction and social pressure.'

Julian sighed and rubbed his nose. It was insulting really, because I could see there was so much he wanted to say and that he was very tired already.

'It sounds like a good thing and maybe it is in many parts. The struggle of individual will against social pressure is more pronounced here, like it was for us, especially women, years ago. But, you know, is it better? We've taken our ideas very far, to the extent that we are not just free individuals, but isolationists as well. When we can, we have our own rooms, we choose internet echo chambers and the right to self-determine all values as if our beliefs wouldn't affect others, as if everyone lived in a vacuum. And society condones that.

We were walking back down through the forest and he stopped still. He looked me in the eye. Before he spoke, I could see this was close to him. Maybe this was the reason for his sadness. It tied to his attempts to reconnect with his roots here, I guessed.

'Is that not a cause for concern? Do you know that there is a completely different way of talking to people here? It's determined by the vocabulary of a family... You see in English we always say 'you' and 'I' to pinpoint a person. That's an accurate metaphysical distinction, as in it says where I start and end, and where you start and end. They're words that act as an outline. 'You' and 'I' exist here, as in the concept of yourself, as removed from other things, exists. But nearly always, people will call you by the title you would hold in their family. So you wouldn't say 'you' to me, you'd say 'brother' or 'sister' if I was a girl. And you'd call a woman your mother's age 'aunt' even if you've never met her before. And you'd call a young child 'child' and refer to yourself as 'uncle' in relation to it. Do you see what that means?'

'No.'

'It means that even when people are talking to strangers, they describe that person in relation to themselves. It means that people acknowledge their relationships even in passing moments. There is the functional distinction that you are a person and I am another person, but the way of speaking here says that a person exists in relation to others, not just themselves .... Isn't that important?'

He looked at me for confirmation that he had hit home and that I wasn't just being polite. It was important to him and his brow was furrowed. I nodded and closed my eyes slowly to imply gravity and understanding, but I had departed. From that first notion of architecture, a thought had risen from my depths and, as it came up, I had begun to recognize it and its constituent parts.

As we drove back into town, Pater and Vera were sat in my head again. I felt how Vera, like Julian, had pleaded with me to see how she saw the world, and maybe I began to, in nations

94

which are constantly built and dissolved, their personalities warped by the fluxes of age, like we are too, like Julian's Vietnam or Pater's Italy. And the nations in us are a discordant multitude as well, calling for harmony from their disparate corners.

What understanding I could negotiate between my voices I didn't know. After we returned to Saigon, I recognized an old feeling beneath the static, bound to that summer and Vera, but that was something I had wanted to escape.

And one night I escaped quite far.

It was sweaty and neon-y as usual. Someone had paid to play 'Inspector Norse' for a second time and the DJ took the money, shooed him away and took a long drag on his cigarette before looping the song on YouTube. The guy went back to his group of tank-top-shorts-Air-Force-One boys and girls in tasselled tops, yoga pants or jean shorts, and dishevelled hair. The boys' hands awkwardly jabbed forward, touching the girls on the hips and trying to act as if they didn't mind their friends hitting on the same girl at the same time. The girls patted their feet on the ground whilst shifting from one leg to the other in an elephantine movement. A Vietnamese waitress, who couldn't have been much more than 20, pushed a middle-aged man's hand off her shoulder as she gave his table more drinks and left. They laughed and called after her in English. A young bartender tried to speak to a group of guys who were trying to take photos with him as he gave them buckets of cheap spirits and mixers. One of them tried to open the little door that led to the back of the bar and then the rest of the staff came to tell them that wasn't all right. At another table a bald man in his 60s in a tracksuit sat with two girls in their 20s, who looked at their phones while he sucked on a large balloon filled with NOS and ran his hands down their backs. He sweated and smiled emptily, his eyes almost gone to the back of his head, and his turkey neck cushioning his chin when he closed them and hung his head. In the bar next door, a huge girl danced in front of a passed-out man and her friend filmed it all. A tall white guy put his arm on the head of a shorter Vietnamese man like an arm rest and laughed when the man shook him off.

And it was all so horribly ugly. Just ugly and grotesque, like a crossover of the Beano and the worlds of Ralph Bakshi: childish old men, ugly sex-seekers, jockish thrill-seekers, druggy spiritualists and every class of manqué. We were all here by cowardice, pretending to be adventurers as we crawled over a town like parasites. Ours was an incubated society, far from the local people who we didn't understand, whose culture we took advantage of, whose dignity we trampled with dispassionate excess and disregard, contributing nothing. We were insular, like me in my head, concerned only with ourselves, and lying to ourselves to make it better. I thought why I had left home, and I thought of the men walking through Paris and what I should see now. Mind-less, self-excusing opportunism, cowardice and cruelty. And I understood the cruelty finally, even those cruelties I had not meant. 'Art is a priesthood', Vera had said. Or something like it. By this time, I was already forsaking such a call-ing, my Adam was almost spent, but that senti-ment throbbed in my head. I saw it in the world Julian had described to me and felt the burden of guilt for my own selfishness. Staring between my feet, the instances showered down in thousands of moments of wilful self-regard, among which one was a truly awful thing. I had left Vera. I had left her, and she had needed me. It was simple and painful because I had known it before I left and did it anyway. More than known, I had felt it. It was urgent that I see her again.

The girl next to me turned to me with a con-spiratorial smile. "I told you it was good. I can really feel it now."

Bedevil yourselves! So that time will not burden you! So that you won't be martyred to it! That is how we seize control of time, the only way we know to warp it and change its passage. And there is so much to get drunk on. I think music akin to drunkenness. I feel it when I fall into my mother's arms after a long absence, when my limbs shake, tears flow, and my knees give out beneath me: it is as if I would die of pleasure.

I spent three days in bed. The crapula of machine-gunning hangovers, coffee and noodles had caught up to me. I excused myself from work and barely managed to leave my building, except to get food, drink and pharmaceuticals. It had been my mistake to associate with a group whose energy never ran out. No batteries; they were plugged in at the mains, and I started to suffer for it.

To comfort myself, I tried to find the feeling of elegance of John Cale again and re-read *The Quiet American*. One of its passages struck me that I had not lent much attention to the first time. It read that the Vietnamese language had a musical quality that I had not experienced to that point. Karaoke and public singing are very popular in Vietnam; I had heard people of all ages singing at birthday parties and in their living rooms, in daylight and at night. The whole country sang, but I had not found the music to my taste. I had noticed that most singers rarely held a note. When a long note rang, they accompanied it only for a short duration then rose or dropped. I attributed this to amateur singing, like my own. I was never a good singer and couldn't hold a note either. But I investigated it further to find out what exactly was so musical about the language, being that I was burrowed away and often bored. I found the reason for these musical breaks soon enough. The language has six tones, of which only one is a flat sound, where the vowel is not twisted up or down during pronunciation. So, it was difficult to hold a note, because so many words required an inflection to be pronounced correctly or they would have a different meaning. Perhaps Graham Greene knew something I didn't, but it seemed to me a language that was difficult to sing as it was made of short words, lunging in different directions.

After that, I started developing some more thoughts about music on paper:

I've been listening to the Beach Boys again and thinking why popular music is so terrible now compared to then.

Wouldn't it be nice if the music was better and had more intellectual, thematic and compositional integrity like Brian Wilson? I'm waiting for that day and have a small theory on how we ended up here.

In the 1980s, synthesizers became widely available and cheap to buy. I imagine this really screwed up the average quality of musicianship worldwide. Where previously an artist would have to learn the wiles of an instrument and develop an appreciation for complexities of musical character, anyone could come up with 3 minutes of song on a synthesizer, and increasingly they have. Hence all the tack of the 80s and since. The ranks of amateurs have diluted the real musicians. I know people say there's no accounting for taste, but I think more people should be held accountable for their lack of creativity and integrity.

The following night, I drank quite a lot and com-
mitted more chaos to paper.

*We imagine the beginnings of man. Out of
the pheromones and spiderwebs of animal
impulses, a light plays down the walls inside
our head. That glimmer lights up some of the
mess inside and we become conscious and self-
aware.*

*Early man, at the dawn of his life, had the
same faculties of understanding we do, I think.
How are the clouds made? How does the water
flow? How does death come to exist? Without
the benefit of millions of lifetimes of refined
observation and understanding, it seems obvious (even scientific in a way) that man should
invent a more powerful being to explain these
things. It would be impossible to conceive of a
physical explanation, and after all, early man
would already have a plausible answer. Consciousness, the same light that raised him from
the animal up, must be the power that made all
these great deeds. A house is built through will,
a baby is conceived through will, so why not a
cloud or water, or life itself? That consciousness
should be the origin of existence is not a new
idea, I know. Notions of 'prima causa' exist in
every religion, I think, so it was a reasonable
placeholder for the origin of all things and a
harmonious one, being that it gave authorship
to powers beyond our own, and the comforting
notion of a deliberate orchestration of existence.*

Music (notwithstanding modern tastes for dissonance) is an intelligent, conscious effort for harmony. When we examine it, we search for the meaningful interplay of elements that would otherwise be disparate. We feel how one element supports, accentuates, refines and enhances another within a structure and the result is something greater than the sum of its parts, delineating beauty, purpose as one note leads us through time to the next one. 'All art tends towards the quality of music' I learned recently, and that seems truer to me now. We seek harmony in all things: the flavours of wine, the interactions between people, the processes of nature, black and white. Where it is, we appreciate harmony, where it isn't, we might project it all the same because that is nicer.

It is this effort that leads me to associate music and any thoughts of a conscious, deliberate cosmogony. The cyclical passage of water into lifeforms and back, and other models of a balanced system, are a sign of this. But it is a false equivalency, because there is no conscious creation there, unlike the music. Or if there is, I cannot feel it. Malcolm's death was a disturbing reminder of chaos. Now when I observe any worldly harmony, I remind myself that it is the harmony of birdsong, not music.

We still grow up in a world that is marked by our beliefs in spiritualities and gods, where we associate a frisson with something other-worldly and enjoy the uncanny. But there is nothing uncanny. We are a teenage civilization, wanting and seeing the need for independence, but reluctant to leave the comfort of infancy and the feeling of care over us. Faith is such a poisonous idea, compelling us to deny evidence and follow our confirmation bias that we will be preserved, as all animals blindly wish to be preserved, through all their pheromones and spiderwebs.

From: Passim Cephalophore

The day after that I recognized the downward spiral I was replicating like a fiction that needed an apotheosis. Vera had been right about me and the book. I was acting like the tortured man that appealed to an old me. It had a taint of *Herzog,* certainly Greene and Vera and things no longer organic to me. I was descended from that person now, so it was time to go home.

Before I left, Julian sought me out with a text message: 'Where have you been you diamond geezer?'

I invited him over for a drink and when he arrived, I explained myself. He said "Wow, you look like shit. Maybe you're right to go home."

I nodded. I told him that it was for the best that I get out of limbo.

"Well, sure you gotta go home some time," he said. "*Chơi xong đi.* Sounds like you miss your parents... And your aunt."

I hadn't meant for that to come across.

He sighed: "When flowers are hard to pick, he spoils who tears them from the tree."

And that was the last time I saw Julian.

The *Relais* is the place I went to in Saigon. I booked a flight home shortly after that night and ended my sojourn with with a celebratory meal. It was very easy to be dramatic when drunk, and I enjoyed what it stirred inside me. I thought of Robert Smith who thought the best rock was written before a musician reached 30, and so wrote *Disintegration* during his 29th year. I had often thought of others who had achieved so much before my age, like Justin Bieber and Newton... I found my way back to Matthew Gregory Lewis who attained literary celebrity in 1796 when he was just 16. There was also Anthony Burgess who only started scribbling properly in his late 30s when he had death in his head. His example was comforting, but I didn't know what I should do next with my life anyway.

Maybe, I thought, baldy, dead, old, gay Walter Pater was wrong as well. All art should tend towards the condition of good food, which had as much artistry and harmony as a song, and as much power to move; after all Proust found seven novels inside some cake. There was the real art: a substance that sustained the physical and spiritual man. Whatever blues can be felt a meal can tend to as well as a song or a book, and it united people at a table, which is music.

A parliament in my head screamed to distance

myself from this fruitless theorizing. And one of them I imagined was Vera, my very own ship on the hill. Some time had gone misused in my attempts to follow her, for reasons I had not questioned for very long. I was melancholic in temperament and slow to move. I had been an obsolete person for too long, and to twist myself out of him now, by whatever way I could bend, was daunting.

My drink was almost empty, the fat man's plate as well. He licked his lips; the mix of thick sauce, saliva and wine made gluey, squelchy sounds. The fatso snorted and broke the food bit by bit; his body a thick, writhing pink paste, his dark head pulling here and there like a maggot. I wanted to shout, "You're going to die, humongous pig!" and tell him to stop this blind destruction of beauty. He belched, and his body lifted the table beneath him, spilling wine over his table, but he fought on, grabbing his victim by the bone, pressing the meat's juices between his fingers, coating them in its varnish, his gooey slobber-tongue milling it in his open mouth splashing over with red wine. A mute scream rattled my head and bones; to leap over and shred the features of his face with his serrated knife, flay the skin, break his head in two at the mouth and pummel a fistful of his eyes, hair, snot and lard down the slopping red hole. His wriggling, dying tubes would splutter and spit their last, gurgling food, wine and bile, swamping warmth around my feet and my toes wiggling and clenching delightfully. But

I just paid the bill and crossed the alley through the puddles and rain on jittery legs, choking on my fettered shout.

11

Where did the time go? No account of it is satisfying.

The houses, fields and roads wobbled into focus, then it was delightful to breathe the cold air again and to hear voices and meaning in the conversations people had, especially my parents. They were overjoyed as they picked me up and hugged me and tousled my hair. On the way home we spoke about my short excursion and what I'd seen. I told them it was another world, but it wasn't, it had been my world with cheaper beer. That was the truth, though I didn't tell them because I didn't want them to be disappointed.

We went home and prepared a vast breakfast of beans, eggs, toast, bacon, tea, black pudding, tomatoes and sausages. Within no time, we picked up where we had left off and I loved it. In fact, I had not known how much I could miss it. I told them stories about my trip and a few tit-bits about the small elements of life I had noticed were different. Perhaps they were accurate, and likely my parents would never now the difference if they weren't.

After we had finished our food a silence came,

and my mother and father exchanged glances. She said it.

"Have you spoken to Vera, dear?"

I shook my head and mumbled no; Vera hadn't answered the few times I had tried to call her. But somewhere in me I had already guessed what would come. In one long, quivering breath, all the air left me as she spoke.

"She's been taken to the hospital and... Oh, it's awful. She has gotten a lot worse since you left."

Her eyes sank to her hands, wrapped around her tea. My father looked at us both sadly as he tightened his lips to keep bean juice from spilling out. He poured me more tea, shaking his head as my mother continued.

"She was as truculent as ever when they were taking her in of course and her doctor likes her very much. They're always talking about her spirit and fight. She's been ill for a long time though, and well it seems it's all catching up to her now. That's just how it is. Age moves in unexpected turns and at a certain point, when something goes wrong, it affects everything. And Vera is old now."

"But she's not so old!" I protested.

My mother looked at me. Her brow had softened and calmed, but it was not meant to comfort me. She was composing herself in resignation.

My father moved more food around his plate. I nervously twiddled the teaspoon in my hands and saw the warped, pink-white puddle of my face. I wondered if I could have seen, had my face been

106

contorted like it was in the spoon, like the Ele-
phant Man. But my parents were waiting for me
to express something more about this news, so I
dashed the thought away.

"You will go and see her at the hospital, won't
you?" my mother asked. "You know how much
she loves you."

Of course.

That same afternoon, I was asked to help with
the preparations being made for Vera's departure.
The house in Wimbledon was gutted, as it had to
be. What feeling of permanence I had attached to
there, a sense of ownership and belonging, had to
be dismissed. Slowly we broke our ties to it, wan-
dering through the rooms, salvaging heirlooms
and curios. We collected her photographs and
her albums, and I put every painting of hers in
the car boot. My parents said there was nowhere
to store them all, but I said I would find a way.

I was hesitant to enter her room. I was told
to fetch her clothes, but I didn't go immediately.
For a while, I sat outside the door and thought
how I had never waited in this spot, only ever
gone through it. It was the sort of thing you'd
only think of when you have to say goodbye to
it all, otherwise such a thought would have no
significance. But in this time, when the curtains
were being drawn, I wanted to commit it all to
memory. I kept the bed clothes from my room,
'but you can't sleep in them again,' I remembered
on my way to see Vera that evening.

The hospital was complicated to navigate. The jaundiced colour of the walls and medical and sick smells in the air were unpleasant and progressively worse with each step I took going further in. I deliberately avoided asking for directions to give myself time to think as I wandered in random directions, pretending I was unwillingly lost. But there was nothing to think about and nothing to solve to feel better. More than anything, I felt the emptiness of my head as I avoided thoughts of the inevitable.

I meandered a good while before I stopped my performance and asked to be shown to Vera's room. A nurse led me that way and I felt steadily more dreadful as we got closer.

The breath caught in my throat as I opened the door but, to my relief, she was asleep. She looked so different: her face had grown heavy with wrinkles that layered over each other, and the skin glistened with an oily sheen like she was made of candle wax. Her hair wasn't styled anymore but lay down her back naturally. The grey suddenly looked very old, where before it had been offset by wonderful forms that stole the attention. On her arms, the skin had sunken and exposed dark veins. Her long, once elegant fingers were now gnarled, sallow and swollen like a monkey's. I had never seen her so still and weak, nor so dispossessed of majesty. She looked helpless, fragile and childlike.

I stayed at her bedside for hours, my head laid by her leg. But she slept and slept, until my eyes started closing too, then she laid a hand on my cheek.

In her last days, Vera had only a few moments of lucidity and it was painful to see the dwindling fire in her eyes. On those lucky days she spoke to me about plans I was making for my life and turned all conversation away from herself. When I asked how she felt and things we might do together, she recovered the old iron in her blood and stopped me resolutely. It was futile to pursue these conversations about her, but I wanted to pretend because it seemed impossible as if the world had moved on from her. Just imagining the words twisted me around a million ways. Instead, I spoke to her about new work I was looking for and how I had given up painting. I tried to soothe her by laughing and saying I never had the talent she had. But it was incorrect to play to her ego, because it had started to leave her already.

"You shouldn't say that," she said, going soft in that way I had rarely seen. She was lying up in bed, her face turned to mine. She didn't have the strength then to lift herself anymore. Every part of her was going silent.

"I always thought what you did was wonderful."

"Even my Eton mess?" I said with a forced smile, choking down a confused whimper for her compliment.

"I don't know why I always spoke like that, I'm sorry. Do you forgive me?"

"There's nothing to forgive," I insisted truthfully.

It took some throttle, but she pushed the painful memory down and, when her eyes opened again, she smiled, like it would banish how she felt.

"Thank you. It's nice that you had some time to see the world. I think it did you good."

But I couldn't see it. The steady hum of Vera was diminishing with such astounding speed and soon it would be gone from my life. It seemed insane to have laughed and blithered so much and to have sought air when she was so close to the earth again. How could I think it was time well spent? Eternity was almost on her, this source of infinite, fading wealth. And less than a week before, I had been high out of my mind. How oblique.

The last time I saw her, Vera and I went for lunch. I wheeled her out of the hospital with pride and we went through the park. And there we saw a wonderful small thing, recorded in an instant. It was two mothers: the first had two children running around her. She kept touching them on the head as they passed and followed them with her eyes. All the while she spoke with another mother, a few years younger, who held a baby on her lap. I think the younger mother was receiving advice from her friend, because she kept looking at her own child and then at the two running about them. She looked helpless, lost and confused, like she was trying to process some vast calculation. She was older than me, but she looked like a teenager again, angsty and insecure, hoping to hear something to make it all better, and find what she needed for this little being she had occasioned into the world. Vera saw them and smiled, and she squeezed my hand.

We went to a restaurant afterwards. Food was brought out to us and I ate with youthful gusto, but then I saw that Vera was in difficulty. She pushed and cut at the piece of meat on her plate, but she couldn't get through. She sweated and worked on mutely, her face strained and humiliated. She tried not to shake the table but there was no relief and other guests started to watch. It was pitiful to see because it was so simple: she couldn't feed herself, and as she fought this indignity, her embarrassment grew, and I felt her shrink to an aspect of animal febrility. I tried to help her, but she didn't want me to. People at other tables pointed, but she felt worse when they had noticed, abandoning her struggle and cowering lower in her chair. The gestures from around us grew and grew until I stood up and shouted violently at the waiter. I demanded another meal and declared what we were given to be revolting. I said the smell was enough to put her off and that they should bring us something less shameful. And when I sat back down, I tried to resume the thread of feeling we had taken with us from the park. I put her jacket over her shoulders to cover the sight of her sweat and threw fire at the others to look away.

When we returned to the hospital, she looked near dead and I tried to pull her back to me one last time. Just once more I wanted to see the light in her eyes, to comfort her against this traumatic eviction. I took her hand in mine and told her that I loved her the most. For all the good my parents had done for me and the love I had for them, it was she who had built me, and that I was her son too. Her mouth quivered, her eyes closed, and she turned her face away, struggling to breathe. I gripped her hand tighter to impress on her that it was true and convince her with my conviction. I could not figure anything else to help her. She needed me to show her that she was not over, and that I would carry her onwards. When she looked up from my hand gripping hers, she couldn't speak, but calm was coming to her as I had never seen, and gratitude that she would never be able to express. When I left her, I had to think very long if I had meant what I said. Against my own will, I concluded it was a lie, though for a long time it had felt like the truth. Maybe it touched her that I tried, but it would bother me for a long time afterwards to think that the last thing I told Vera was a lie, even one I meant well by.

Two days from then she was gone. Her illness caused her a great deal of pain, and she boiled with despair as it slowly extinguished her, but she also fought against hopelessness, even when she knew she could not hope for hope. It upset me very much that she died so badly, as Malcolm had.

My father was asked to give another speech and he said all the right things. He spoke about her heyday, when she had had the greatest recognition, and found a kinder way to imagine the last two decades of her life, when she had become reclusive and spiteful. It was always his disposition to see the best in people and that quality helped me through Vera's funeral.

It was an unusually bright day as we trundled into the graveyard. In a way I had hoped for grey clouds and rain, because I thought it would have pleased her to go under severe circumstances. My cousin Francis said she was a "just such a good person, you know? So wise and we will always have her in our hearts." I don't think Vera would have liked to be described in such TV sentiments, nor that it was true. I could not really say that she was a good person, it was more complicated. She had tried to be good and tend to the world by painting it in its true colours, but whatever mix of problems swilled in her head, she never truly got over it. 'Good' seemed wrong, but I patted Francis on the shoulder gratefully anyway and told him that Vera and I had spoken fondly of him. It made him smile, but later I annoyed him by asking why he had eaten that pig feed as a child. I couldn't contain my smile as his face sank and he started mumbling his awkward answer of "I was just a kid, all right. I don't know." That was Vera in me, niggling him like that.

The sun shone on that cold day. On the other side of the grave, I saw Rufus who nodded at me sympathetically. Despite the pants incident, I guessed we were still friends. Then the priest started. He looked a bit tired and spoke with false sincerity about the soul and I wondered if his heart was really in it. Maybe there were lots of priests who lost their faith but kept going because it was a job like any other. I wondered what other jobs the priesthood qualified one for. Priest turned city boy? No. Priest turned insurance salesman? Kind of the same job. Priest turned politician? Very familiar to history. Priest on the dole? Why not? He was only human and if I had thrown in the cloth, I might need time to find new purpose as well.

When the service was over, we went back to Vera's garden. We raised our glasses and drank to her memory, saying one last goodbye. And I have enjoyed what passed, but the music ends too soon.